ACE SCIENCE FICTION SPECIAL 5

FELIX C. GOTSCHALK

GROWING UP IN TIER 3000

"You're six years old, Jonas, don't be a dumbshit. There is no room for you *and* your putative parents on this facet of the planetoid. The energy in this billet-piston is constant only when two organisms couple in for it—it's magnetic, and magnetic energy is bilateral, symmetric, duetic. Any tertiary drainage sets up dissonance—and guess who's the tertiary in your house. But you're getting stronger, and I'm going to stay right here and help you——"

"What about your putative mother?" Jonas asks.

"Well," Carol cuts a look at the wall isochronon, "my sixth putmot should now be in a great many icky pieces."

"What did you do?" Jonas sounds excited.

"It's almost slapstick. I put a bottle of nitro on the garage door transom. Now we can work on your putpars—we *do,* my pony, or we *die.* . . ."

FELIX C. GOTSCHALK. Born 1929 in Richmond, Virginia. BS '54, MS '56 psychology, Virginia Commonwealth University. Doctoral work at Tulane '57-'58. Taught psychology at Nicholls College in Louisiana '58-'62, a psychologist in North Carolina since '62. Married, two children. Weight-lifter, pianist, composer, poet, model-builder, painter and inventor. Author of 35 short stories, a novelette and one novel.

"I live in moderately stultified setting made bearable by Bach, four old Mercedes Benz's, a grand piano, an Eames chair, and richly variegated memory-trace varibles, Dostoyevsky is a god to me, and I would like to write like Henry Miller, Edward Albee, HL Mencken, GB Shaw, and a little like Kafka. As for writing itself, it is something I do for me. If people "like" what I write, fine—if they don't, it's no skin off my ass. I would like to write something that would be truly influential, something that would change peoples' thinking for the better, make them more humane . . . but people have short memories."

FELIX C. GOTSCHALK

GROWING UP IN TIER 3000

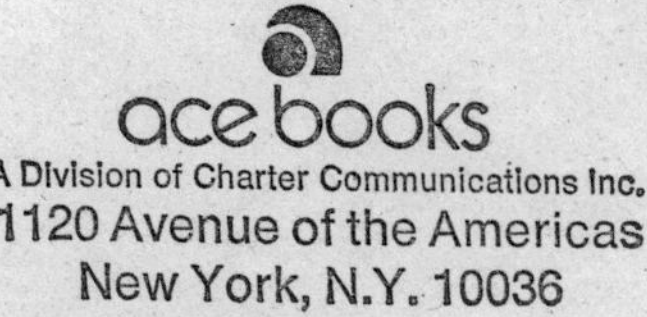
ace books
A Division of Charter Communications Inc.
1120 Avenue of the Americas
New York, N.Y. 10036

GROWING UP IN TIER 3000

An Ace Book

Printed in U.S.A.

I

The sticky golden sunlight pours over small Jonas, like a cone of bright honey. He is sitting on a slick wooden chair, his legs flat against the warm surface. He looks down the short length of his thighs and calves to wonder at the shine of his patent leather shoes, angling them apart like pincers, then clicking the sole edges together like hedge clippers. He spreads his fingers and feels the pancake syrup seep into the webbings.

At the breakfast table, close by his chair, a materno-surrogate is sitting, legs crossed casually, a newspaper very close to her dull, non-faceted eyes. She is pheno-typically humanoid, but with several cyborg implants and holobot prostheses. Jonas is supra-humanoid, and wonders why this fat lady-thing is not doing anything interactional.

"Hey-hey," he vectors, "hey-hey", and sees the form start behind the spread pages, "I be Jonas Sum Ex to the thirty-seventh power, loci Alpha—you wish to play with me?"

The newspaper half-drops and half-crumples, revealing a brown anthropoid face, rock-like eyes oozing a dull glare. A puffy prehensile digit-prosthesis dips clumsily into a box of chocolates and hands one to Jonas: "Quiet be," the lady-thing gruffs, and Jonas feels unhappy emo-sensor radiates.

The ingress chime duns a crisply choffing consonant in his audiosensors, followed by a pleasing psychophysical tone. Jonas slides flat onto his back, does a quick turn to starboard, feels the slick wood all over his ventrals, then begins to slide off the chair: the size mini-beta eee patent leathers first, then the fat calves and the fatter thighs, the blip of a bird-in-the-bush genital bud, and the resistant nudge of the rib-cage against the brink of the precipice. Now the little body is off the chair and levitates the final inches to the oiled rosewood decking.

"I investigate ingress vesicle stimulus!" his voice blooms out like a *trompeta real*. He toddles toward the front of the house. "Back come, little creep!" the materno-surrogate blats out, the flat tone infused with an abrasive raucousness.

"Ram it up your exhaust orifice—if you have one!" Jonas blats back at the rising form, and fluxes on a protective isomorph as the thing beams a stunbolt at him.

"Corporal shithead!" Jonas screams, as the light bolt bumps him up against a pilaster. "Assaulter of minors! child abuser! back to the scrap pile, hive of Mitsubishi circuit paks!"

"I answer door, you bad boy," the form waddles off.

"Who the royal fuck programmed you?" Jonas taunts.

"Bad boy" the thing shakes its head, "horrible little Alpha brat."

"When is my putative mother coming home?" Jonas calls.

"Anytime now."

"Who codes for ingress?" Jonas follows the surmat to the bulkhead vesicle, trying to see around the wide undulating hips. He gives up and activates his X-ray probes.

"Carol!" he exhults as the vesicle irises open and an interestingly pretty red-haired five-year-old girl waves at him. The child is optimally puffy-faced, with sad alert eyes and a nice purse to the set of her lips. She palms her ID trivid cube snappily into the surmat's thoracic slot, then seems to pout as the ingress force-field fades slowly.

Jonas pushes around the elephantine surmat and opens his arms to the small girl; he looks ready to embrace a haystack or carry a barrel. "Carol, Carol, Carol!" he sings in differential stereo tones, embracing her skillfully, "I couldn't have wished for anybody else!" He places his hand gently on her cheek, and kisses her, as if biting into a honey-dew melon. Carol returns the quick ardor of the embrace, then she sits on a chaise and stretches, luxuriating.

"Shameless Alpha kids," the surmat mutters, rolling down the hall like a ship wallowing in heavy seas. Jonas walks in playful menace up to Carol and leans his high cerebrotonic forehead against hers. Several seconds pass, then Jonas says softly, "your emosensor readings are beautiful—how are mine?" Carol responds, opening her mouth in charming oral receptivity, then chewing lightly on Jonas's lip-corner. "Good, good, good," she says, between the tiny chewing nibbles. "I've missed you. Why haven't you come to my billet to play?" Jonas angles a thumb toward the hallway. "My guardians have me saddled with a goddam clod of a surmat—can you imagine such grovel? I can't override her force-fields. Worse still, she's shot full of punitive motive-tropisms. Shit, I say Good Morning Mam, and she draws back her stun-bolt latch——"

"You shouldn't swear so much, Jonas."

"Why the hell not?"

"It's not adaptive."

"Adaptive—aschmaptive, it's adaptive for me."

"I do wish you'd try to stop."

"Well I don't want to."

"It would make me so happy."

"Why should you care?"

"Because you do so well affirm my feelings of self-worth, and elegant verbal content sweetens the potion all the more."

"Well, I like to swear. It's anal-expulsive, erotic, even erogenous, it's androgenic, and it's cathartic—so fuckee, fuckee fuck fuck fuck." Carol covers her ears with her hands, but smiles coyly all the while; then she hugs Jonas very quickly, vectoring in a subtle hypothalamic azimuth-tickler.

"Let's play something," she sounds affectedly pouty. "Race you to the promontorium deck!"

The two children dart for a porthole set high in the wall, flitting like quick birds nesting in the face of a building. They levitate in different azimuths, wriggle through the circular vent, and scuttle up through a squirrel-cage ladder. They emerge onto a deck of neutral flat gray, extending elliptically forty feet wide and twenty feet deep. Chaises and valve-stem chairs are scattered in random patterns on the floor. An environdial console is against a central pillar, like an ancient theater organ, its stops and buttons and tablets winking dimly. A softly luminescent geodesic dome canopies overhead, the filter slattings set to control the heliofires from the ring of sombre orange suns at ten o'clock high.

"Want to laser some pterodactyls?" Jonas perks.

"I'm tired of shooting things. I know—let's wrestle a black cat!" Jonas looks smugly disdainful, then agreeable, as if he is going to let less favored neighborhood kids slide down his rain-barrel. "Okay," he says, "but only if we dial him up nice and big."

He vaults up on the console bench and scans the rows and arcs of controls, activating two heavy double-throws and a cluster of rheostat-type dials. The console hums, whines, whistles, then soars silently to ultrasonic ranges.

"Let's see," Jonas muses, "I always have to figure this out—remember the day you dialed a turtle, and it came without a shell?" Carol giggles and does a slow fluid somersault on the deck.

"Get some nice rugs," she asks, and a matting of resilient tight mesh materializes beneath her. Jonas's fingers stray over the controls: "TAXONOMY, ABSTRACT RELATIONS, SPACE, PHYSICS, MATTER—here we are. MATTER: *Inorganic, Organic, vitality, vegetable life, animals*—here! *primates, reptiles, snakes, marines, cetaceans, fish, birds, poultry, horses*—where the hell are the felis catus? Goddamit, this is a slow environdial——"

"Be patient, baby, and talk sweet."

"*Cattle, sheep, swine, hogs, dawgs*—hey, here's a gazelle hound—wonder what that looks like? *Cats! breeds of cats*—at last! Now, what breed?"

"Burmese."

"Here goes," Jonas presses a clavier-like key, dials a rheostat to LIFE SCALE, and presses three buttons.

"Kitty kitty kitty," Carol squeals, as a compact feline form begins to materialize on the trivid deck: its color is a rich, warm, sable brown. The coat is fine, glossy, satin-like, very close-lying, and the eyes are gold-colored, deep, brilliant, expressive. The face is subjectively sweet. Jonas dials the cat up quickly to lion-size and hops off onto the heavy rug. He flings himself on the cat's back and Carol hugs one of the huge forelegs.

"You don't need the protectomorph," Jonas calls down to her, "he's set for low hypothalamic amperage." The children pummel and prod the big cat and it responds in slow motion, rolling over on its side. They dive into the silken flanks and grab tight little fistfuls of soft hair, writhing like dogs in grass. Jonas bulldogs the huge head. Carol sprints to the console and sets an audio control. The cat mews like a dying siren and the children laugh in piercing high-frequency cries. They seem to tire quickly and nestle into the belly like suckling kittens.

"Where is your putative mater?" Carol asks absently.

"Gone to another of those sociologic nostalgia sabbaticals."

"How about your putative sire?"

"He's been in the homeostasis spa for three days. I think he's getting old. How about your parental figures?"

"Pater's assigned to gladiator school this month and mater's in a topologic bridge tournament." Jonas nestles his face against the purring warm expanse and hugs Carol in a dorsal-spoon posture.

"I feel lonely, Carol. Sometimes I feel lonely even in a room full of deferrent comrades, or peers, or even competitors or symbionts. Even when I am the sociometric star I feel lonely. I wonder if supra-humanoids have always been lonely. Do you sometimes wonder why we are even here on this planetoid?"

Carol looks surprised and restless. "Goodness, no—I try not to do the imponderable bit. I mean, infinite regresses are not my bag of kindergarten-level input. Do you take your amphet blatters with your cereal?"

"Yilch!—yes, but then I come off of the perceptual high like a house of cards, every day about dinnertime."

"What dosage do they have you on?"

"Fifty milligrams."

"Why do we have to take amphet anyway?"

"You know—to make us feel good."

"Wouldn't we feel good anyway?"

"I don't know."

"Have you ever missed your amphet blatters?"

"Once when the housebot got cross-phased."

"What happened?"

"I waxed sad and masochistic. Then, about ten that morning, the municipal satellite flew over the house and I felt better all of a sudden. My putative pater said the whole city-environ is radiated daily with some brand of happy rays."

"Shouldn't we both be feeling extra good right now?"

"I think we are, really. But still there's something unnatural, if that is the right word, about feeling good or homeostatic or euphoric all the time. It seems to take extra effort to be intellective about it. Right now, I feel like I'm holding my hand on an old phonodisc, slowing its rotation just a tiny bit, but knowing that it would be ever so much easier to let it spin at its geared speed."

The surmat's flat mask appears in a wall visoplate: "What children do?" it sounds both interrogatory and voyeuristic. "You behave or get stunbolt."

"Yay, ugly!" Jonas crows. "Say, where'd you get your face—in a used phsiog mart?"

"Hush Jonas, don't make her mad," Carol whispers.

"Not let big pussy piss on rug," the voice is whiningly admonishing.

"Well, if it does, I'll be sure and call you to bring a large mop," Jonas laughs. "Hey, Miz Surmat, Lawrence Welk is on the trivids. You said you wanted to watch him—remember?" The surmat looks puzzled, the wide mouth opens, a vague flicking of surprise stirs the physiog plate, and the screen goes blank.

"You square old bitch! Hopper of Grannies! Flaccid tiddies!"

"Jonas, Jonas," Carol sounds urgent, "my, what language. Please, come, hug me. Be still, that's good. Be quiescent. My, what an angry boy!"

The children lie face to face and embrace each other. The effect is that of old people embracing. There is no clumsiness, no embarrassment, no sexual connotations, no passion; rather, the children cling together like frightened primates. Their small hearts beat strongly, but on different sides of the ventral bond. Jonas closes his eyes, but feels bristlingly alert. His eyes snap open and he activates his holographic x-ray probes.

"You have lovely parathyroids," he giggles, locking his thighs around her in a tight scissor-claw.

"Naughty precocious man! Suppose I peeked at your gee-yew tract?" Carol teases, kissing Jonas's eyes closed with little flicks of her tongue.

"Go ahead—tell me what you see." Carol nestles closer and activates her probes.

"I see billions of microcosmic pearls in precious tight zygotic wreaths. And, I see a beautiful little chestnut, and an epididymal coil like pure silver thread and, yes, vesicles of superb resilience, and a urethra like a golden cornucopia."

"You say it so well, so poetic, so wholesome," Jonas looks moved, then his eyes glint with fierce playfulness. "Why, you're as wholesome as a goddam peanut butter sammidge."

"Oh, you ruin it, Jonas," she squirms in his grip, "and besides, you're not nearly pubescent yet. Your sex goodies are deep down in the cookie-jar—hey, let's find something good to eat." He releases her and they stand up. Jonas dials the cat off, scans the dials, and says, "you pick something—say, do you know that before cannibalism and syntheticism, we ate only animal meat and by-products and botanical foliage?" Carol nudges beside Jonas at the console.

"I remember trying to eat baleen strips and tundra grass once, when we got dialed into the polar cap environ. It was spooky. But I cheated and dialed a candy bar and some brandy. Well, let's see here, how about some generic comestibles: a little cup of borscht, heavy on the cream, a light saddle of mutton, and here's one of those heavenly embryonic *cochonette de lait* piggies

—yummy and supra-yummy! And how about a brace of squab?"

"You're my little squab, aren't you?" Jonas nuzzles her cheek.

"Yes, yes," Carol sings, warmly breathless. "*You* act as an adequate reinforcement contingency for *me,* and *I* will be *your* darling contingency of reinforcement." She looks over the slowly turning menu readouts. "Now for some bread—no ethnic disdain now—here's some matzoth——"

"You sounded clinical as h—ah, very clinical, all that talk about contingency reinforcements a minute ago. It hurt my emosensor." A long tenuous silence ensues. "Do you . . . ah . . . love me, Carol?"

"I don't believe I heard you correctly."

"Do you love me."

"Christ, I haven't heard that word in years. What a question! And look, you made me say something inelegant—yum, here's some eclairs, they're always good . . ." Carol turns as Jonas begins to cry. "Goodness, what's the matter? Don't you like eclairs?" Jonas slides onto the deck into a fetal position. "I want somebody to love me," he wails.

"There, there, baby, Carol loves you," she hovers over the small form, "whatever has come over you—wait! I see what's wrong—turn over!" Jonas rolls flat on his back. Carol spreads the mesh at Jonas's umbilicar medallion and adjusts the silver bezel. It snaps with an authoritative, spring-loaded thock. "There. Heavens, your homeostasis tap was loose. You were leaking self-pity, plus other icy vectors and vapors. How do you feel now?"

"I bet that shit-eating surmat loosened me with that sneaky stunbolt," Jonas bounds up, jogging and shadow-boxing, "I'd like to ram a soldering iron up her solid-state panasonic ass!"

"You're hopeless, Jonas, wherever did you learn such language?"

"Same as you. From the books and discs and tapes and cubes——"

"You've been digging the restricted pornies, haven't you?"

"Hasn't everybody?"

"Well, I don't know——"

"Come on, Carol Baby, my little ptarmigan, all that jazz is public domain. It's yours for the dialing. My swearing is bush league—you should dial some De Sade on the trivid, or some random Inquisition samples."

"Let's be elegant though. It's ever so much more fun."

"I need a bite—an *edge* to my input though. Elegance is pithy, maudlin, ephemeral——"

"It can be soothing, leavening, engorging."

"Tell the truth now—would you rather wrench a gemsbok thigh with your canines, or bite daintily into an eclair?"

"By far the latter, my pony, but come on, the dinner is coming, let's eat, and talk too." The children sit on valve-stem chairs next to a wall panel.

"Cold beet soup!" Jonas whines playfully, then smiles an all but evil leer, "but good!" Carol winces, recognizing the punch line from the old moose-turd stew joke. They eat the food carelessly, Carol seeming to try harder to be sedate at the counter-ledge where the dishes lay. In the bleak distant vista, a huge tornadic stack forms and moves in. Jonas's billet-house gets immediate warnings and the gold colored unit sinks into the concrete, like a huge piston being lowered into a cylinder. The kids gorge themselves and wonder what to do to liven things up.

II

"Conflict, conflict, goddamned conflict," Jason 262 mutters through his soft blonde beard, "all I ever get on my emos is conflict—what's your emo reading, if you don't mind my asking." Ellen 715 stirs in her impact field as the terracar hisses along the intra-commune azimuth. She looks about 35, blonde, shapely, substantial, nondescript in physiognomy.

"I've been keeping mine shunted off lately, dear," she says, "except when I'm around people who I think are going to give off zapping good vectors." Jason looks surprised. "I tried that once. Shunted out about an hour of bad static and auras at Lon's and Kat's one night. But when I opened the channels later, it was like getting octopus ink right in the face."

"I know," Ellen nods knowingly, "I usually try to time it with a euphorion spansule, or sometimes with a coma nap. It makes it a little easier."

"You fat little doll," Jason teases, "have you ever cut the stuff loose at orgasm?"

"How ever did you guess, momma's sweet stud?"

"It came through like muriatic acid in a cream soda."

"Romantic analogy, king of kings." Jason notches the steam to mach .21 and angles the car onto a delivery trench stretching out toward the empty horizon.

"Ah now, that felt much better. King of kings eh. Thanks. Say, maybe the iso on this car is getting thin. Driving through the megalop is like wading in sewage."

"Yilch, that smudged my emos," Ellen rolls away in mock aversion. They laugh, sigh, and dwindle into silence. The car hisses holistically, as if the entire planetoid was being thrust through the ethers by one slow macrocosmic steamtide. The sound is inherently tranquilizing.

"We're almost home. What are we going to do about the kids?" Ellen asks. "I honestly think we're going to have to do the Hansel and Gretel bit," Jason sighs, "Jonas will be at the patricide stage in a very few months now."

"Don't forget matricide," Ellen shudders, "that little Carol is deadly. She stuffed a grandsire clone into the ration-maker the other day."

"And she's so sweet with the physiog bit and the expressive manner."

"Whose idea did you say it was to obliterate superego input anyway?"

"God, that's ancient history. The trivid archives show that a pediatrician named Ben Spock IV got the aerosol cut loose."

"Well I say damn Ben Spock, and double damn the cumulative effects of his Id aerosol," Ellen sounds tough and cynical, "and triple damn Ben Spock III, Junior, and the old man especially."

"When you dig the goals and not the means, you *innovate*," Jason quips, but weariness shows in his tone, "if we're going to last in this societal rat-race, we've got to ditch the kids one way or another. Say, you mentioned Carol. Her father didn't make it at glad school—went into the fire-trough this morning."

"At least that's a quick way to go." Ellen shudders again. "A kid out in Pacific Shoals skewered his putfat on a meathook and hung him in the freezer."

"I half suspect that Carol's father went into the trough on purpose. You know, Carol's almost gotten him a few times. She notched the steam valve on his car last week

—used a coping saw. The car blew up in the egress port in the middle of the night." Jason shifts in his impact mesh and stretches.

"I had an idea about twenty years ago—a nutty idea, I thought, but it kept nudging at me. Can you guess what it was? Of course you can't." Ellen smiles tolerantly. "Listen now. My idea was that mental age becomes entirely and absolutely independent of chronological age very early in life. And I mean early, like four, five, or six. It's easy to say now because the evidence is all around us: the four year-olds are like young bucks, the five year-olds are peers and competitors, and the six year-olds are goddam predators. I broached the idea to my major prof way back then, and he smiled smugly, and went back to polishing the udders on his sacred cows."

A light pulses on the control facings and a force-field envelops the car. "Stunbolt coming!" Jason does not sound particularly urgent. They stiffen in their impact amniotics as the bolt hits the car from four o'clock medium. A fuse indicator flares and smokes and the air-conditioning wisps into silence. "Goddam kids," Jason spits.

A mile away, six young boys laugh and pummel each other as they train a rifle on another terracar. "My putfat used this for elephant hunting," one giggles. Three decks below, the boy's father twitches slowly on the floor, his emphysema implant melted by a vector-bolt summated by the six boys.

"How far to go?" Ellen asks, easing a Mellarino under her tongue.

"About five kilos."

"Good."

"Shit, we have dominion over nothing," Jason says fatalistically. The car hisses through the glowing trench, the wide tail lenses pulsing caution flares. Under the louvered hood, a tiny spume of freon leaks from the compressor-adjunct. "Anyway," Jason snaps out of his gloom, "I had this feeling years ago that some young kids were brighter than adults—and not just relatively brighter. Absolutely brighter. It would have been untenable to say that a four year old with a 150 IQ was directly comparable to an adult who tested at 150—the indices of measurement were vastly different. But then, we began this saturate bit, flooding the kids with compressed input day and night.

"Do you realize that Sam Bowman's four year-old out-reasoned him just last week? And on the subject of the anthropological division of labor! Sam told me it was just something he had never heard anything about. Then the kid asked him something like, 'do you think your contributory societal worth justifies your organismic viability?' "

"Does that mean what I think it means?" Ellen's incredulity is laced with a pressing fear.

"Yes. He was saying, are you good enough to keep on being alive? Sam's scared to turn his back on him. He keeps requisitioning stronger surmats, even a provobot for one weekend, and tries to stay out of the house."

The car angles up imperceptibly and begins to lift clear of the trench, easing parallel to the glowing road-bed and sliding into a toll booth lock. Jason irises the vesicle on the driver's side and punches in an address code in the face of the booth control panel. The car eases down an access ramp and up a quiet street reprod flanked by tall trees and fleshy foliage. In front of their billet-piston, a circular door opens, like the lid on a giant trap-door spider's nest, and the car slides into the recovery conduit. It emerges into a garage-like cavern and stops. On the ledge, two small figures bounce and clap and squeal greetings.

"Daddy-daddy!" Jonas trumpets. "Yay for my big putfat and putmot!"

"Yippy-Ki-Yo-Ki-Yay," Carol says softly.

The gull-wings lift slowly and the parents look up apprehensively at their six year-old son and his five year-old playmate. The children seem to be sizing up the adults like puppies in a basket. Their little eyes gleam down intently at the weak-looking pair.

"Too pooped to pop?" Jonas's voice has a taunting edge. "Here, mommy-boo, let me help you." He turns to a wall panel and rams the levitator control into a shift-gate. Ellen bumps up suddenly, her shins scraping the instrument panel cowl. "Ouch—careful, baby, I'm not as young as I used to be." She lifts ponderously onto the ledge and Jonas hugs her warmly. Jason looks up to see the boy nuzzling Ellen's genital area with mock innocence.

"Give old putdad a lift, will you, son?" Jason calls. He flexes on an isomorph as Carol moves toward the levitator control. She pushes the lever down smartly and snaps it into the shift-gate. Jason feels the buoyancy of his body and the ultrasonic tingle of the force-field as he lifts out of the car. He starts as Carol playfully notches the levitator rod out of the gate, then back very quickly. It is like a trap-door opening on a gallows platform. But Carol beams a wide smile and says, "Oops! I didn't do it right, did I?" Jason settles on the ledge beside Ellen. Jonas grabs him by the thigh. Jason actually wonders if he may grab him by the testicles and twist them like a dishrag.

"Did you have fun at the homeospa, daddy-boo?"

"My putfat's at the dumb gladiator school," Carol

says, her tone somehow mocking virility. Jonas puts his arm gently on the little girl's shoulder, and she luxuriates like a cat being petted. The response throws Jason off stride.

"When are you supposed to go home, Carol?"

"Who knows, surrogate putfat pussycat," she giggles, "nobody's ever there."

"Hasn't anyone called for you?"

"Negative. What's the big deal? My house is swarming with automated gimcracks and at least two surmats, at last count, but I got out. Nobody knows where I am."

"Is your mother due in tonight?"

"Only if she loses in the tournament."

"Let's go upstairs and relax, I'm bushed." They step into airlifts and sift up through the shaft to the main deck. The children bound out in quick somersaults while Jason and Ellen sink into chaises. The surmat comes rolling up. "Bad children——" it starts to bleat, but Jason waves it silent. "Thank you, Nell, but we're very tired. You may retire and go on non-verbal."

"Shall keep scanners open?" the surmat looks a bit furtive, its eyes moving from the children to the adults and back. Jason looks up into the flat brown face and reads its concerned expression.

"Well . . . yes . . . if you like," Jason tries to sound casual.

"Will sit on charge pod in corner—maybe sleep," the surmat waddles across the room, flinching as Carol feints a jab at the huge belly.

"Carol," Jason begins, trying to sound serious and kind at the same time, "I'm afraid I have some rather bad news for you." Carol darts over and springs onto his thigh. Jonas is on the other thigh in a flash. The two youngsters beam their bright eyes at Jason, and Carol pinches his thigh with light erogenous skill.

"What's the sad scoop, Jay?" she sounds like a barmaid. "I haven't had any gloom input in days."

"Carol, honey, your daddy had an accident today." The child shows a faint glimmer of concern, but it is more like a flat spot in her bright mood.

"Don't tell me he got boffed at glad school," the voice is whining but clearly detached and disdainful.

"What do you mean, boffed?"

"You know—like zilched, zeroed, ciphered, seppukued——"

"He's dead, honey," Jason moves to hold the child, but she draws back.

"That's what I mean, surro-daddy, deady dead dead!" the voice is intent, then measured and soft, "you don't have to try to be kind. It isn't as if the world's ended. He was my sixth putative pater—shit, now I'll get issued another one——"

"Carol, don't say that!" Ellen sounds horrified.

"Don't say what?" pure tone innocence snaps back, "Oh, *that*—I've been playing with Jonas too much. He talks gross a lot—don't you, Carol's little pony," she leans over and kisses him low on the neck.

"Aren't you sorry about your father?" Ellen looks on the verge of tears.

"Sorrow, my dear lady, is a maladaptive reaction, and I am rarely if ever maladaptive. I had to do the sackcloth and ashes bit on my first birthday, and it has been an annual event ever since. Anyway, this putfat number six was a drag. Shit—excuse me—he was even hooked on mammary blatters. And at his age!"

"You mean he still liked to suck tits?" Jonas perks in.

"Jonas! What a thing to say!" Ellen lifts out of her chaise, trembling.

"Well, it's true." Carol giggles, then sounds matter-of-fact. "At an age when self-actualization and readiness for zilchood were the expectancy parameters, this putfat number *seis* was goddam fixated at oral ingestive loci. He was immature, fawningly dependent, and leaked unfitness like a sieve. He even tried to draw strength from me—my charisma leak is strong . . ." her eyes gleam at Jonas in shared secrecy. Jason ponders at the stream of talk and decides to try another tack.

"Would you like to stay with us tonight?"

"I'd like to stay with my pony-stud, Jonas."

"That's what I mean, honey."

"Say, you and your consort here are a lot more adaptive than most. I could stay with you, couldn't I?"

"The Synod statutes say no."

"Oh, fuck the Synod, and the statutes too!"

"Carol, baby, I do wish you wouldn't talk so."

"Well, okay, I'll try to beam you some relative elegance. That's funny—just this morning, I was bugging Jonas to talk sweet—then I found it to be more cathartic, more adaptive, to talk neuter or gross."

Ellen's face is wet with tears, Jason looks shaken, and the surmat glowers from the corner pod, like a Buddha with dull eyes. Jason probes for abstraction strength, but finds the effort too tiring.

He leans in to both children and squeezes their hands hard, then feels the coiled adult strength in their kinesthetic aversiveness. "Listen," he says, "do you know the old saying, 'come, let us reason together?' "

"Yes," the reply comes in vocal tandem.

"Well, I'd like to reason with you both."

"But you see, there's no reason to reason—" Carol smothers a little laugh with the back of her hand. "That didn't come out right—our behaviors are rigorously programmed and optimally reinforced. Reasoning, as such, amounts to little more than semantic ingratiation. You might stave off your day of ultimate zilch awhile, but you know that it will come."

"But people have always known this."

"Not with the short-term finality in today's world—that sounds corny. Listen, butterflies live a very short, sweet, compressed day. Romeo and Juliet filled their relatively short lives to the brim with honey and vinegar, and died happily. But even then, their concept of psychological time allowed them sweet, unhurried fulfillment."

"You and Jonas can help us to live longer," Jason's face brightens, "I've always wanted to die of old age."

"Oh really now," Carol sounds obdurate, "no one's died of natural causes for at least twenty years—and besides, people in hell want ice-water." Jason sighs. Can this truly be a pretty little five year-old girl talking?

"About how much time do we have?" Jason knows the answer, but feels basically uncertain.

"I'll be a predator real soon!" Jonas sings out. "My teleconsolbot told me I'd be able to drive, maybe even teleport or multilocate—if I turn out to be superior." The boy sounds proud as his eyes beam up at Jason. Show and tell, Jason muses bitterly, what totally innocent little Machiavellians.

"I'm precocious," Carol says saucily, "my puce-hued consolbot keeps blatting out little cards with TS messages punched in them."

"TS?" Jason says, then remembers the answer too late.

"Tough shitsky!" Carol soars, slapping Jason's thigh, then slipping neutrally into a matter-of-fact tone, "the cards say that I'm at critical mass on my input parameters. Well, an old putmot of mine—she's deceased now, rest her putative soul—used to say I was too smart for my training britches. And I never even had any training britches—shit, that's intra-ute conditioning—hey, I made a Freudian slippy-poo! Hey, two of them!"

Jason feels grieved in a way he has seldom been before. And, mounting above the sickness of his sorrow is the knowledge that he must fight, plan, be on guard, be supra-paranoid, in order to stay alive another year.

"Goodness me, do you still have an iso on?" Carol teases, pinching Jason's wrist.

"Yes, baby, all us old men wear them."

"Why, for heaven's dear sake?" Carol sounds wonderfully naive and child-like.

"The better to prevent charming little things like you and Jonas from slitting us like cantaloupes."

"Pretty-pretty!" Carol gives a little high scream, holding up both her hands, as razor-sharp metal talons erupt from her fingertips. "How ever did you know that I had a new implant? You geriatrics are just worlds smarter than you used to be!"

Ellen stands up and smooths her mesh sheath, nervously. She looks both frightened and determined. "Well, let's have a long truce, all of you. Jonas, Carol, you know you can't get through our isomorph fields; and you know that our energy reserves are still strong."

"However decremental," Carol sounds teasing.

"We may as well have fun together," Ellen says lamely, but the children look notably unmoved. "Well," Ellen fights off a thick sob, "you might as well let *us* have fun together."

"Not many ways," little Jonas shakes his head. "Hey, Carol, I saw a trivid the other day about Eskimoes. They have a neat societal way of seeing to it that the young get all the goodies. The old Eskies have to walk straight out into the cold and get zilched. I mean like dead ahead, permanent azimuth, toward the pole, even!"

"Youth must be goddam well served!" Carol sings in blatant facetious tones, giving a double-armed black power salute. On an impulse, Jason grabs the child in a heavy bear hug, as if hoping to quiet her, or soothe her into quiescence, or hold her until she has agreed to be kind and docile. Carol hugs him quickly and whispers rapidly in his ear: "I like you anyway. Say, you could even deflower me—I'll be pubescent in about six months. How would you like that?" Her chrome talons flick out and one of the awful tips traces along Jason's pulsing jugular. "You could build up, say, one—no, two weeks continence maybe; then, take a double aphro and do with me as you wish. Then, when your orgasm peaks, and you're all surging hypothalamus and itching spinal reflex-arcs, *then,* I could rip your corded blue jugular like a machete across a high pressure hose."

"Precious infantile bitch!" Jason manages, "that would be worth dying for!"

"I want to hug my father!" Jonas pouts, reaching for Jason. Carol slides onto the deck and Jonas hugs Jason. The embrace feels ventrally genuine, but Jason knows that the warm snuggling muscle tonus will turn to striated purposeful extensor vectors rapidly.

"To bed, to bed, little pony," Carol tugs at Jonas. He slips onto the floor and the two skip across the wide decking and flit like birds into a receptacle and up a shaft. A porous silence settles over the geodeck.

III

"Hast thou done the deed?" Carol cups her hand to Jonas's ear in the dark hall. Jonas feels a déjà vu glimmer, then ties it quickly to trivid Shakespeare, and smiles casually. "Their bedroom vesicle is triple-laced with force-pads, and has a timer lock, set for the morning, I guess. Anyway, I couldn't get in."

"How did they look?"

"Sleeping like babies. Mother's got the intravenous Mallarino flowing and Dad's doing the cool gelatin cocoon bit."

"What about the surmat?"

"Picked up her signal once, but it was weak. She's probably down there on her fat warty ass with her ancillaries disconnected." The two small figures slip through a bulkhead cleft and into a bedroom. The bed looks a floating tablecloth of microfilm. The children dive onto it and move about like bears on rubbery gelatin.

"I don't want to kill mommy and daddy yet," Jonas says, petulance coloring his intellectuality. "I know you don't, baby," Carol is consoling, "but you *will*. Don't worry so—you're getting better every day, and I can help you a lot." She nestles beside him and speaks softly and intently. "We have to work toward global invulnerability—you have to get your implants and prosthets operable. But, just as important, get familiar with weapons—we have to make very goddam certain that *they* don't get the drop on *us*."

Jonas crackles a bite of potato cube and drains a glass of ale-concentrate. "Would old putpate really try to do me in?"

"Your inputs on that index should be firm by now. Maybe you have some mild developmental retardation. How do you feel? And how's your umbicular implant?" Jonas looks at his navel, perhaps wishing he could contemplate a genuine dimpled invagination, inny or outey, and holds the metallic bezel like a doorknob, turning it ever so slightly. "Feels okay," he says.

"Well don't be a dumbshit. There is no room for you *and* your putative parents on this facet of the planetoid. The energy in this billet-piston is constant only when two organisms couple in for it—it's magnetic, but you know that—anyway, magnetic energy is bilateral, symmetric, duetic, dichotomous. Any tertiary drainage sets up dissonance—and guess who is the tertiary in your house. But, you're getting stronger every day, and I can help you really complete the new abscissa-ordinate pocket—you *do,* my pony, or you *die.* . . ."

"You sure are smart, Carol."

"You'll be just as smart soon, and after all, it's no great feat of a cap-feather for either of us. We are getting full-saturate cybernetic input all the time. We are the fucking products of the information explosion!"

"What about your mother?" Jonas seems to remember something.

"Well . . . unless the old nitro gets flat with age, my sixth putmot should now be in a great many icky pieces." Carol cuts a look at the wall isochronon. It reads 4:50.

"What did you do?" Jonas sounds excited.

"It's almost slapstick. I put a bottle of nitro on the garage door transom."

"But, won't the provobots be after you now?"

"Negative. I planted a clone of dear sweet little me beside the door. I too should now be just so much piquant pediatric mincemeat."

"You're going to stay with us then?"

"You got it, baby."

"You know, when my parameters fatten up, I am positively going to ravish you. We are going to soar together, fuse our tactiles like hot tar babies, and spear and skewer and baptize each other. You're really quite a prize." Carol kisses him quickly. They lapse into sleep like disconnected dolls.

Outside, a cold albescent rainbow bends low into the craggy western horizon and the six iron-red suns skew up in the east. The rays sweep across undulating green oceans, onto wet flats and salt marshes, up the soft curves of dunes, and across deserts. With barely half a degree elevation from visual horizon, the rusty orange light moves inexorably across tundra and filigree, bogs and foothills, fissures, faults, mountain ranges. The light dances briefly on the sensor atop the billet-piston where Jason and Ellen and Jonas and Carol lie asleep inside. The house begins to stir.

Ellen's deep-primed coma nap ends, electrodes drop away from her temples, and the intra-vene lead retracts into its cochlear shell. Jason stretches luxuriantly in a coffin-shaped mass of greenish gelatin. The visodome irises open and the energizing light falls weakly into the room. Ellen stirs and smiles at Jason. She autovectors Mozart sonatas. Jason feels asymmetric and dials Scriabin. They lie quietly, waiting for the initial homeostatic inputs. Ellen reads dulled synaptic gaps (due to mild thioridazine addiction), estrus nadirs, and moderate anxiety state. Jason reads crackling hot synaptic proline, wide-spectrum vitamin deficits, bristling tumescence, and flexible paranoid nuances.

"Can we tolerate strong isos all day?" Ellen queries.

"Affirmative."

"Well, let's get the kids off somewhere, anyway, and

try to lose them. Did you get the visotape on Carol's mother?"

"Yes. A messy way to go, but again, quick." Jason taps into the children's room: "Hey kids! Come on—let's take a ride!" Jonas and Carol watch the visoscreen fade.

"They're going to try the Hansel plus Gretel bit," Carol says, almost tolerantly.

"At least they're predictable," Jonas shrugs.

IV

"Did you ever see a killer wasp take off carrying a locust?" Jason nudges Jonas. "You mean a cicada killer?" Jonas sounds corrective. Ellen and Carol sit behind them in the air-cushion hovercar. "Yeah, cicada killer," Jason sounds corrected. "I once saw one lift off across a patch of hard ground. It looked like a heavy plane, ponderously taking off, stirring a tiny rooster tail of dust . . . the way we're flying right now reminds me of it."

The vehicle speeds over the flat red desert like a fly scudding over a pool table. Jason notches the control stalks back and the craft begins a shallow climb. The racing red flats drop away slowly, then stop. The vestigial delta wings glisten a wet silver. Jason punches in a flight plan and eases back to semi-recline.

"Where are we going?" Ellen asks.

"Thought we'd take a spin up to tundra parallels, maybe higher—Okay with you, kids?"

"No preference," Carol says quietly.

"Can I laser an iceberg?" Jonas asks.

"Well, maybe a small one," Jason laughs. The craft banks softly, then begins a steep accelerating climb, pushing the four forms deeper in their impact-neutralizing mesh. Levelling off at 100,000 feet, the ship picks up speed toward the polar cap. The desert gives way to sharply buckling mountains, softly soliflucted expanses, then pingos, oriented lakes, and polygons. The ship prescribes an optimal Gaussian trajectory, arching down in a positively decelerated plane, to skim a blue-white glacial ribbon.

"We'll go back at tree-top level," Jason says. "Hey,

that will be a real visual blast," Carol sounds openly enthusiastic. The car skids to a long slow stop and the gullwings snap open, the pure icy air immersing Jason, Ellen, Jonas and Carol in tingling compact crystalline molecules. To breathe the air is to be intoxicated. "Want to jump out?" Jason says to the kids.

"Yay—go!" Jonas trumpets, defluxing his impact-mesh and clambering over the side. Carol follows him. The gullwings close authoritatively, snagging a corner of Carol's sheath. She quickly defluxes her clothing and pushes Jonas hard into the snowcrust as Jason guns the terracar down the glacier.

The backwash from the JATO pods scuttles the children along the surface like bodies washing onto a beach, but they cling together like twins in a clear bubble, safe in the amniotic force-field. They sit up in the snow as the terracar appears low up-glacier.

"Christ, I didn't think they'd dump us and strafe us both," Jonas says hoarsely, feeling for his transport implants. Photon-beam pods lower from the terracar's fuselage as it begins to pick up speed. "The transport implants will be too slow," Carol says intently, "do you have any teleport energy?"

"Barely sixty KVA."

"This will be like two men sharing about one and a half parachutes, but hang on. . . ." Carol grabs Jonas full around his neck, cants her legs around his waist, and activates her teleportation implants. The children hang high above the glacier as the terracar sweeps over the ice, with dusky orange photon-cones falling on the surface like strobe-lights. "I should be scared shitless," Jonas whispers to Carol, "but I'm not—when did you learn to do this?—it's supra-great!"

"I don't think they'll see us up here." Carol looks steadily at the craft far below, "looks like they'll do another slow pass—no, goddamit, they see us—listen, I'm going to teleport us onto one of the mountain tops—hold tight. . . ." Carol wrenches a rheostat implant in her tricep, and the children are instantly knee-deep in snow, on an 18,000 foot peak. "Now, be still, and I'll opaque the force-field," Carol says, "they'll never find us here."

"How the royal fuck are we going to get home?" Incredulity edges into Jonas's voice. "No problem," Carol says lightly, "I taped the flight plan. A simple vectorial reciprocate input will put us back in good old Morton Groves, Illinois Sector. We'll probably have to stay here a day or so—we need massive solar radiation to compensate for your retardation—goddamit Jonas, do you have any idea how many seven and ten year-olds are bugging me for consortial access?"

"No." Jonas looks very glum.

"Well, very damn many—but wait, I didn't mean to sound cruel—it's just the situational stress. You really do reinforce my autoworth better than anybody else. Come, taste the snow, and kiss me. . . ."

The force-field amniot is like a warm sphere around them. It sinks slightly into the snow as they embrace. The terracar booms away softly, trailing a vapor-line in the brash blue metallic sky. Jonas feels a surge of protectiveness in his small chest. He holds Carol tightly and whispers little nonsense things to her: "If the big deistical cat wanted to show a delegation the sweetest facet of the planet, he'd point at you. When can we conjugate? I want to bend you like a tungsten spring and skewer hot bolts into the fissure halving your succulent globes. I want to set your pelvic floors throbbing and your organism soaring like a hundred peregrines. I want to feed you orchids and truffles and the rarest distillate nectars. I want to weld my mouth to yours and seal your cathedral with mushroom stalks. . . ."

"Sweet talk, sweet, sweet," Carol sighs, squeezing Jonas possessively, "and true extrapolation. But, listen now, we have to get all our sensors out and zeroed in. We'll have to stay here, but that's no big hassle. We're going to need fat reserves to get back, unless we can flag down a freighter or beam onto a municipal satellite. . . ."

"We seem to be on a ledge. Don't we need a better campsite?"

"Negative. It's just a few minutes before noon. We can stay here through the night, and *maybe* lift off in mid-morning, depending on how much reserve KVA we can build up."

The children lie flat on their backs and orient their sensors towards the suns directly overhead. Carol's frontal lobe sensor does a slow dextra heliotropic turn, and her ventral pods and plates shimmer like burnished gongs. Jonas lies spread-eagled, looking determined and masculine. He has more buds than sensors; but, as he feels the warmth and support of the suns and the amniot, new itchings spread over him—his levitational implants mature precociously, and his physical power fulcrums firm up, as striates replace fatty protein chainings.

He wonders if he will get a hellish sunburn, but Carol says no. "Don't worry, baby, everything noxious gets neutralized in the iso filter, and everything goody-good-good gets let in—just like cool fresh air after a four-hour bridge game. Try to sleep." She rolls onto her stomach. Sensor planks blip into three-dimensionality in her small trapezius muscles, and complex circuitry appears on both latissimi. A banding of antennae appear at the waistline, the cilia waving expectantly. Transport implants show in fine definition inside her sturdy calves. Like sunbathers, outlandishly plucked from the beach, the two children bask in the hot sunlight, near the top of their world.

Five-hundred kilos south, Jason curses, "All the stops are out now—we may have to move out."

"Such sweet-looking children. . . ." Ellen's sadness sounds classic.

V

The suns boom up over the candy white mountain peaks, a row of bright pearls behind serrated teeth. Jonas stirs, a hamster in a nest of wood shavings. Carol lies awake, supine, a waxen doll, her pupils pinpoints of irical black, as if any additional light energy would be disallowed entry. Jonas feels the softly whirring tension of her body and wonders at his own feelings of strength and mobility.

"When will we be ready to blast off?" he asks Carol, yawning, overtly unconcerned. Carol is silent for a long minute, then lets out a long whistling sigh, nestling against him. "We can teleport almost any time now, but I think we ought to wait for one of the asepsis satellites. We can beam up to it easily, and its unmanned, so we won't have any new putpars to worry about." Jonas stands up and stretches, then falls back in a playful supine spread eagle. "Man, that feels good," he says from the soft ground-level mold his body makes in the new snow, "this feels like being fitted for a personal iron maiden."

Carol stands and looks out over the mass of sharp-topped mountains. Her eyes notch to 50X and she scans the horizons. "Commercial freighter at one o'clock low—we don't want that. I see a wedge of fighters doing the contour sweep bit at three o'clock very low and into the foreground—can you see them?" Jonas tries his binocular power but it is fuzzy in resolution. The fighters are reverse-delta stabs. "They look like wing-nuts flying backwards," he says. "Slow satellite at ten median," Carol says guardedly, "maybe we can snag it." The craft passes at about 20,000 feet, like a spidery spoked wheel. "It looks hot," Carol says. Then, scanning closer, "It *is* hot—radioactive plus some cosmic clummocks."

"I'm hungry," Jonas sounds dimly plaintive, and Carol hands him a fatty protein hormone synthete from her umbilical band. "Hey, no gustative cues, but instant satiation," Jonas says, feeling his stomach wonderingly. The children sit in the snow and deflux their amniotic isos. The air seeps into them like embalming fluid and Carol motions for refluxing the protective isos. "We remain helpless naked apes," Jonas sounds Byronistic "God, I felt like a fetus in ice water—hey! I don't believe what I see—look!"

Far down the glacier, like a fat bug struggling up a conveyor belt is a bush-plane reprod, yellow wings bold against light blue fuselage and rudder, with yellow stabs and floats. The radial engine chatters laboriously and the craft seems to be moving at less than 100 mph. "Dry-as-dust nostalgia," Carol says, admiration faintly coloring her incredulity, "who the hell would bring a antique reprod aircraft this far up?" Jonas looks fascinated. "It's somebody with a wild and old nostalgia cube doing the Alaskan bush-pilot bit," he says. "I bet he's friendly——"

"Nobody's friendly," Carol notches in quickly. "This may even be a trap to get us out into the open."

The plane labors up the frozen ice-filled valley and skis to a long wavering stop. It begins to slide backward, then turns sideways and stops. The tiny door opens and a man jumps lightly onto the ice. He is wearing a checkered mackinaw, heavy boots laced to the knees, and a cap with loose ear-flaps. A large Husky pack dog leaps out, barking excitedly. "Hey, let's go see——" Jonas sounds naively excited.

"It's a goddam demolitionary android," Carol grates deep vocal chord rasps, her binocs set at 100X. "I can see the fuses strung around his fucking neck. You can bet that this is a present from Jason and Ellen, your ever-loving putpars. We're supposed to rush down to the kindly old Sergeant Preston Yukon daddy-symbol and say like, Gee, can I pet your big dog? And he'll smile and plock the detonating rods to critical and blow us all into assorted pieces."

"Can you get close enough to set off the stuff with a stunbolt?" Jonas begins to sound like a platoon leader.

"Negative—unless the explosives are as old as the rest of the scene. I'd have to take a big bet that it's sophisticated stuff, like hydrogen extract or maybe cobalt."

"It's localized though," Jonas says, "they wouldn't send a cannon to kill a sparrow, and think what this must have cost them in barter parameters—what a contract!" Carol looks thoughtful. The android and the dog circle the plane slowly and look occasionally at the walls of the mountains. "About as subtle as a turd in a punch-bowl," Carol says, "they probably have us on a trivid screen monitor, or at least we're reading on their sensors, so we are expected to show ourselves."

"Couldn't the pilot just gun us down when we, uh, if we get within range?"

"He's programmed to know our strength. I'd say no."

"What are we going to do?"

"Get down there, wait for him to make his move, and teleport just before detonation."

"That's cutting it very damn close."

"Theoretically, we could get off in a fraction of a second."

"Just how obvious can we expect his move to be?"

"He's got to be fairly open. He won't know when we're coming, or whether we know he is demolitionary or not . . . wait, let me try something."

Carol falls softly prone, like a Marine boot at slow fire at 500 yards. She rests her chin on her hands, forming a bipod, and ellipses her binocs to maximum. Her view scans over the android face, the neuter-bland physiognomy, the slash of aminoplast lip-line, the faceted eyes, the quad orifices of the nasal prosthete. Auditory shells are visible under the ear-flaps. Carol struggles to get resolution of the picture, the greatly magnified yoke of fuses and plastic trinitrates focusing and refocusing in the periphery of her vision. "Shit, he's going to have to light a match to himself to set that off—we might have guessed really that your putpars couldn't swing a cool sure-thing demo contract. We'll be safe enough to approach him and teleport, say, right back here, when the fuses go."

The small forms begin a little slalom down the slopes, their levitators easing out the rough spots and the transport implants muffled down for braking. They ski onto the glacier and drift toward the plane. The android waves as if flagging down a train and the husky bounds out, bushy tail wagging. Jonas slides up to the polished wooden prop, with Carol bumping him gently from behind and closing her hand firmly around his life-support waistband. "Gee, mister, what a keen plane. . . ."

Jonas feels like toying with the android. A pasty hand reaches up, almost in clumsy haste, to turn a knurled valve, and blue sparks fizzle across the android's neck. Carol tightens her grip on Jonas and activates her teleport implant. In a delicious soaring moment, they are back on the mountain ledge. The android fumbles frantically with its thoracic energy cells, then is obliterated in a bright starburst of dusky orange light. One yellow wing whips up through the smoke and cartwheels slowly back down, bouncing and cracking on the ice. A blunted whooshing explosion rumbles up to the childrens' ears.

"Scratch one android character actor, one 1930 model radial Fairchild, and a form-fitting bomb," Carol says vacantly.

"And the husky." Jonas sounds sad.

"Getting the drift of the war we're in?" Carol sounds masculine.

"Yeah. Say, was there ever a time when groups were cohesive because of positive bonds? You know, did people ever dig each other to the extent of showing routine cooperation?"

"No."

"I somehow expected a more extended answer."

"I can give you a long no or a short no."

"Do you see conflict as adaptive?"

"Again, adaptive-aschmaptive. You fight the heat or leave the kitchen, and the latter amounts to wasting your chances. If you are a sick reindeer, you belong to the wolf. If you're imperative about your territory—hey, I made a funny—you gut it out till your putative parents either move out or get zilched."

"We are very much like animals, aren't we?"

"Shit, we're not nearly as good—good in the sense of orderly lives. We have grown intellectually arrogant and purport to deny instinct as somehow beneath our dignity. Try baring your little white neck to Jason or Ellen and you'll get it slit. But the wolf, ah, the maligned, feared predator, pisses on the ground beside the bared neck of the loser, and shows some brand of instinctual compassion—hey, how did we get on this subject? We can intellectualize at the colloquia—let's get off this scary perch and try to get the drop on the parental pair.

They probably think we're zilched by the former Sergeant Android Preston."

A provobot satellite arcs high overhead. An airsled drops from the gondola and sets trajectory for the smoking glacial crater. The children teleport to the scene and wave as the provobot sled hisses to a landing. The bot stands in Colossus of Rhodes stance, tapes Carol's account of the incident, and takes trivid shots of the area. The robot is squat and nondescript and neutral in manner. He mounts a tiny cycle seat on the sled and motions for the children to get into the storage pod. The sled lifts off toward the hovering satellite.

Carol pinches Jonas playfully. "The provobots will see that we return to our region. They will probably take us right to our tower. Won't Jason and Ellen be surprised?" Carol's giggle spins into a snarl, like a young kitten mewing. "My own dear put-parents," Jonas shakes his head and glints his eyes, "the twin sons of bitches, accidents of the night, fragments of copulatory caprice."

"Now you're getting the idea, baby," Carol says, "we'll have to come up with a special way for them to get theirs . . . maybe something slow and ritualistic, like piranha souffle or carcinoma aerosol!——"

"How about doing a Cask of Amontillado bit, and leave some hydra eggs in the wall?" Jonas crows.

"Crazy," Carol nods.

VI

Jason and Ellen sulk over the topological bridge slab. Jason's sphere is teardrop-shaped and Ellen's is gourd-like. "Henri had a beautiful fat spheroid last week," Ellen moans, "we'll never be good bridge players." Jason tucks his knees up and hugs them tightly, rolling forward slowly in the force-field. "Nobody is a good bridge player," he sounds weary, "at least I never met or even heard of one." They look at the robot dummy's perfect sphere, the cumulative product of perfect intra-player vectors. "Smartass bridge bot," Ellen cuts at the bland face. "Your pleasure, my lady," the pleasing voice replies.

Outside, the territorial sensor atop the region's scanning tower picks up two small teleportational blips. Reciprocal probes beam out and are countered by identification codes. The shimmering blue force-field yields an opening and Jonas and Carol zip through in their silver cocoons. They awake in the sector station like saints in wall niches coming to life. They step from the amniotic shells, small mummies from pure molecular isomorph coffins.

Jonas glances around the station. Two charbots are sweeping the deck with wand-like devices. A large trivid deck is alive with horses charging across frozen Crimean marshes, a small circle of waiting passengers watching in kinesthetic empathy. A noisy familial group emerges from niches across the room and gets noisier when one of the children jabs the putfat with a cane. The rail-thin motput slaps the child with a modstun bolt and drapes him over her hard shoulder. Pure tone symmetric music flows through the transducts, soothing, pacific diatonics.

Jonas and Carol walk toward the egress vesicle. "Let's walk awhile first," Jonas suggests. They flux oxygen packets into their nostrils and emerge from the station onto the mall. A sea of plasticrete stretches out to the glowing terracar trenches. Pedwalks radiate from a central sonic fountain and the air hisses with several aviettes and delivery drones. The suns set fretfully behind a ridge of geodecks, spattering the sky with undulating murky red pseudopods. The children step onto a pedwalk and hunk over in fluid postures. Far ahead, a dowager clone tries to pace her rearing Dalmations, and aft of the children are a group of adolescent copulators on horizontal bars. They admix playful intromissive postures with advanced gymnastic tricks. The pedwalk rolls past a ring of tropical parks and Carol and Jonas step off. They sit on the spongy matting of creeper grasses and look at each other for several seconds.

"I hope this little outing has extinguished your sentimentality," Carol says, her voice yet unsure. "It's more of a shock to some kids than to others, but we have to come to grips with the facts. We have to kill off our putpars. Whatever emotional dependence you felt for them should be waning by now. You probably know this, but I'll say it anyway; you're in a developmental stage in which plateaus and curves, nadirs and asymptotes flow at high rates. One week, you may love the balloon warmth of a maternal breast, and the very next, want to shred it with a razor. You can enjoy paternal piggyback rides heartily, and a few weeks later, you will strain for the tiniest opportunity to get your talon implants around the same neck. The strong hairy hand you like to feel on your shoulder becomes a mail fist to be most seriously feared.

"Life is really rather cheap, you know—much cheaper now than in the past. . . . Sometimes I wonder about all those years before you and I were born—though it really doesn't matter since we have the trivid decks and nostalgia holog cubes. But think how it would have been to live in 1100 instead of 2500, or to have been born an 18th Century prince, or a Kalahari, or a frog—or anything . . . or nothing? It really doesn't matter, and it never really did.

"Despite their *overt* uniqueness, and yours and mine, we are accidents of birth—simple out-and-out accidents. We don't have any goddam *raison d'etre*. We ride awhile on this spinning spheroid, get some kicks, and get zonked. What a stupendous put-on! Everyone was so *sure* there was a difference between the smart and the stupid, peasant and royalty. . . .

"And then anomie arrived on the scene. Did you know that the danger of anomie was predicted as early as 1940? And now we are cohesive because of the autodecimator principle. Who would have predicted that programmed obsolescence would spread to us pediats? And that we would be able to foist it onto the adults?

"I felt unbelieving—really tearfully crushed—when I got my first patricide inputs. I was about four, which is roughly equivalent to the ancient mental age level of about sixteen, and my intellective parameters were beginning to peak. My father, my putfat at the time, was hugging me, and I was getting funny little incest signals. Then I got a vivid engram, bold and blaring and clear: I could see myself eviscerating him with a tiny buzz saw—I felt the actual imprinting! My circuits felt solid-stated, all the synapses in the maze coalesced, baked instantly to porcelain. I felt kinesthetic cues, body English, I grunted, and gave a little lunge. It was like unzipping him from neck to dick, and then wet meaty things fell out. I gagged and he hugged me tighter. I think he knew what had happened.

"We can play and fantasize and live in trivid flashbacks, and we can get great pure hedonistic kicks, and we can feel almost any way we want. But, my favorite little pony, our destiny is to kill our parents. . . ."

Jonas listens and a pterodactyl labors past on groaning leathery wings, pursued by a six year-old in a flitter. Borealis streamers glimmer faintly in the darkening sky. The air smells of musk and pollen, exhaust fumes, detergent, brine, wet fur. Jonas clips fresh packets into his nose.

"We can have the provobots maintain a truce for a few days, can't we?" he says. "I mean, can we do something to ease the pressure—get an insured breathing spell?"

Carol looks vaguely disdainful. "It's possible. And Jason and Ellen would probably buy it."

"I need just a few more days for my inputs to crystallize. I can almost see myself with a third eye, and begin to predict how things will go over the long run. But I'm still a little too much like an intern with his first patient, or a pianist at a first recital, or a nurse learning to give injections." Carol begins a little sigh, but Jonas claps a very strong hand over her wrist. "And don't take any special goddam credit for being advanced in your inputs—just give me a few more days."

Carol starts slightly, and for a brief and charming moment looks docile and engaging. Then the steady predatory glint grows in her bright eyes, like embers being stirred. She squeezes Jonas's hand and blows a puckered kiss at him. "I can feel your strength coursing," she sounds proud. "Maturation transcends training. Remember that pediatric cliché? It's as true as anything ever was. Your experience per se is wholly secondary to your intraorganismic unfolding, your cumulative imprinting. We will wait—and we will make the waiting delicious! Race you home! Transport implants—no fair jostling!"

Carol scrambles to her feet, smooths her leatheroid sheath, and runs teasingly across the turf. She looks back at Jonas's clumsy fumblings and activates her transport implants, lifting off prone, like an albatross. Jonas lifts off and assumes a rudimentary swan-dive position, waggling his short arms as he scuttles off, low over the fleshy grass. Carol autovectors can-can music from her palate stereo implant and ups the decibel weighting to a blare. She skitters through a grove of white aspens, sending the finches up in tiny whirring cones, soars up in a steep angle to about 50 feet altitude, then sets an arrow-straight azimuth for the billet-piston where Jason and Ellen are toying with glowing trig puzzles. Jonas sways behind Carol, like a student pilot jockeying a Piper Cub.

They fly over crumbling apartment towers and lichen-smothered ranch houses; the drill field where 100,000 children were vaporized by the Synod in 2470; the ghetto blocks, all burned out husks of permaplast and astroturf; then the radiating strips of frozen custard stands, dry cleaners, taco booths, chicken bars, stereo modules, copulation globes, and re-cycling plants. They skim the blackened mansard roof of a manor house, set afire in the socio-economic war of 2300. Two Mark XIV's and a Maserati reprod lay rusting in the dry swimming pool. Jonas blats out a surge of anal-expulsive energy and humps onto Carol, dog-fashion. She gives a delighted squeal and spins to embrace him ventral-ventral. They skim over miles of millet fields, truffle grids, and hybrid foliage plots, clinging to each other like mating deerflies.

They land at the community provobot station and requisition two robot bodyguards. They visophone Jason and Ellen and head for home in a terracar driven by the bots.

VII

"Oh, big lumpy clummocks of affectional bullshit, Ellen!" Carol taunts, striding harshly toward the visoport, "it's a wonder you haven't been flicked like a bug. You're maladaptive and weak. . . ." Ellen looks tearful.

"I never wanted to hurt you or Jonas—I love you both, and I can't help it."

"But stop right there," Carol's confidence is luxuriant, "your use of the term *love* pegs you with the color of the flock—the recessive flock, the maladapts. Listen closely to this, Jonas," Carol leans past her slate-gray provobot guard to touch Jonas. "What do you mean, using an archaic and meaningless word like love, Ellen?" Ellen's provobot looks consolingly at her and places a humming pneumoflex hand on her knee.

The children snicker at her uneasiness. "Hey, your bot is empathic, and maybe horney," Carol laughs, "you better try dialing another one." Jason moves to check the bot's registration cubicle, his own provobot hulking after him.

The group looks curiously like a sensitivity training class or an encounter circle. Ellen sits tensely on a pale sonic hassock, her oddly solicitous provobot levitating just off the deck beside her. Its physiog plate turns sombre as Jason snaps its de-phasing toggle and extracts a copper-colored readout plate. "You've drawn a sociologic coddler," Jason sighs to Ellen, "this bot's programmed for domestic court counselling."

"Ours are orthodox bodyguards," Jonas pipes up, "with the response orientations of Doberman pinschers, or better still, parameters from Lyndon Johnson's private security guards."

Jason fights off a brief regurgitatory response at the name. "Well, no great hassle," he says irritatedly, "the protective iso is adequate."

"The ground rules are clear enough," Carol snaps, "we're at an agreed truce, enforced by provobots of matched protectiveness." She all but leers at Ellen. "Tell us about love, Ellen. I want Jonas to get some clarificatory jazz on that subject."

"I've always wanted to be near Jonas," Ellen says sadly, "I wanted just to look at him, and hold him, and do things for him . . . have him near me."

"Why, though?"

"I just did, that's all."

"Isn't it true that your perceptual inputs are richened by Jonas's charismatic vectors?"

"Yes."

"Isn't it true that he reinforces your autoworth parameters?"

"Yes, but——"

"And isn't it true that your affectional feelings for him are precisely mediated by the reinforcement value of his behaviors toward you?"

"I don't think I understand you, Carol."

"Don't you *love* him—Christ, that word bugs the shit out of me—because he makes *you* feel good? Because he reaffirms your feelings of self-worth? Would you love him if he were homoncular, or mutated, or asymmetric, or smelly, or dumb?"

"I don't know——" Ellen sounds squelched.

"Damn right you don't. And it's because your intellective parameters barely get past plus or minus one standard deviation. You've come fairly close to vaporization a few times, haven't you? Like, you can't pull your weight anymore, right? From each, according to his abilities, to each, according to his works. Ellen, my pretty putmot surrogate, you are simply lapsing toward non-contributary societal status. And your espousing love for we who are programmed to replace you in the goods and services matrix is pathognomic evidence of your maladaptiveness."

Ellen begins to cry softly.

"Did you cry when you filled the glacier with laser cones?" Carol grates.

"It would have been a quick way to go," Jason puts in, tentatively, "merciful. Quick."

"You caught us off guard, daddy-boo," Jonas jabs a fat fist at Jason. The provobots all tense and Jonas's fist flicks back from the force-field isomorph. "You could have fooled me—Hey, kiddies, a ride in the country . . . we might even get a coolie at Quik-Pik and eat in the car at Taco City . . . and we can count cows and horsies and play license plate poker and twenny questions—shit!"

"There aren't many neat ways left to go," Jason sounds lame, "neat, in the sense of supra-clever coups. All the Hitchcock ploys ran out years ago, and the Amontillado paradigm has been run into the ground. Hansel and Gretel is not bad, and somebody down the block just did the old Russian Roulette bit. Decided to ease the anxiety and do it on raw chance. And then, one of the kids lost!"

"Isn't that against Synod statutes?" Carol moves in, monitoring the situation like a zealous proctor. Jonas begins to spin lazily in his chair, his feet held high, in a mocking rigor mortis pose.

"The statutes have become largely unenforceable," Jason has the curious tone of a man justifying something by condemning it, "jurisprudence as a significant societal force is largely obsolete. We have no motives to begin to compare with the patricide ones, and since they are both necessary and inevitable, no punitive response is incorporated into the statutes. Because the adults are in decremental stages, and the children surging with increments, it is the old that die, and rarely the young. I can feel my parameters fading even now, and I am sure you feel yours growing. It's the old story of the young strong replacing the old weak."

"Wait a minute," Carol sounds brassy, "what the hell are provobots for anyway—don't we need law enforcement?"

"Think, Carol baby," Jason now sounds beneficent-paternal, and a sliver of smugness edges into his manner, "there is no need for law as such. There are no motives for us to commit *crimes;* in fact, the word itself is sometimes rejected by the newer model semantic monitors. We are protected in an auto-proprioceptive way by our force-screen envelopes. We have no acquisitive motives. Patricide and infanticide are evolutionarily adaptive, and of course, accepted as normal. Scanners and recorders make us open books to each other for the most part. The provobots end up doing traffic control more than anything else. We bring them in for showdowns and crises where full energy levels are being utilized—such as right now. By the way, our high KVA shields, plus these four provos, are costing us plenty on the goods and services index. Look at the energy disc spinning there in the console." Jason points to a rotating metallic disc in the face of a control panel. He moves casually to the console and looks closely at the disc. "Flick off your iso and see the difference," Jason says to Jonas.

"Don't!" Carol blurts, as Jonas defluxes his force-screen, and Jason whips out a small phaser hackbutt.

Jonas's provobot sears the air with a plosive cry and flings himself at Jason. The weapon hums a tight, stringy, cutting whine and cuts into the provobot's epithelial exoderm. The gray form crumples heavily to the deck, then recovers in an instant, and snaps up, nose to nose with Jason's provobot. The raw autonomic responses of the four people autovector maximal isomorph protection, and they stand in a quivering circle, the air seething with hypothalamic vibratos. A tiny spume of sooty smoke sifts from the bot's deltoid cap.

"Hey, very good, daddy—that was really very good!" Jonas's voice quakes at first, then becomes a resonant blare. "You've cumulated a neat thick affectional bond, and I'm still responding to it. Now listen tight and close. You know I can requisition a phaser. All the provos have them. Do you want a smelly hot impasse now? We can wreck the place if you want to go all the way. I suggest we put everybody on auto-pacific code and let the console tractor-beam us for awhile. And we can get some sleep."

"Please, dear," Ellen shivers.

"Yeah," Carol saunters casually to a chaise, "let's cool it and let some quiescence feed through. I need a nap, and now, goddamit, I feel some menarcheal cues—what a time for that!"

Jason backs to the wall, and lets himself slide slowly to the deck, like a collapsing puppet. Ellen hunkers for a few seconds, then rolls to one side, assuming a soft fetal coil. Carol punches the musiform clavier and a crystal of light clangs onto the screen. Jonas drains a champagne goblet and appears to sulk.

"Consensual agreement?" he sings out.

"Affirmative!" Carol trumpets.

"Yeah . . . cool it," Jason sighs.

"Yes, yes, yes," Ellen whispers. The four provobots

move to the center of the console and stand at the corners like pall-bearers.

"Routine auto-pacific code one!" Jonas vectors at the sensor cone atop the console, "tractor-beam enforcement, overide on subsequent consensus only." Each bot punches in a relevant quadrant code: a sighing hum infuses the air and the room feels washed in viscous mist. Tranquilizing particulates permeate the air—sweet, cool, compelling olfactory cues.

The four forms begin to doze—sugared, satiated, swimming slowly in gelatin, embalmed, kissed, baptized, anesthetized. Carol's thoughts probe playfully among her memory-trace variables: fuzzy teddy-bear clones with warm flanks, fences alive with wild honeysuckle and bright striped hornets, frilly dresses and shiny wigs. Ellen sifts through dreary days of boredom, endless unwashed copulation scenes, tiny cups of yellowed gunpowder tea, sackcloth, axillary odors. Jonas's ideation streams with blood-red Ferrari prototypes, grappling irons, lanyard knots, sealing wax, hydras, griffins. Jason's head sags forward, busty nymphs sway toward him and veer away, frosted tankards of dark stout spin slowly, and pulsing saccules flit like darting dragonflies. He plummets from macrocosm to microcosm, red giant to neutrino, blasting down through endlessly telescoping tunnels, the stream of air rippling his brows.

The thick-kneed provobots stand silent, like trees.

VIII

The dusky suns rim up past the visoports. Ellen sleeps deeply on the deck, the effects of four Darvons sluicing through her conduits. Carol spins in the exercise cage like a frantic monkey. "I've come across a Porsche reprod," Jason says to Jonas, with barely enough sincere camaraderie coming through to cause Jonas to attend him. Jonas spares only a bored facial expression.

"It's an S-90 from A.D. '63," Jason leans in, "black, red leather, five on the floor, red-lined at eighty-five, but will go to ten easy. And, better yet, it's a Carrera transplant—twin cams and a flat blower that howls like a Banshee. To drive it is to have it throb in your bones. Want to see it?"

"You said the Amontillado paradigm was passé. What are you trying to pull?"

"Nothing. We can't just sit around on our brooding hostile asses. I thought we'd take the Porsche over to the gladiator pits and watch the action tonight—Of course, there's no room for these hulking provoclods."

"Come off it. I wouldn't trust you to push me to the supermarket in a baby carriage. Is this S-90 in the 356 series?"

"Right. The great aerodynamic teardrop shape, before the in-laws got into the act and vomited the 914."

"What's the format at the gladpits?"

"Dick the Eviscerator and the Danish Transvest Angel, no holds barred."

"What's your motive?"

"No motive. Look, we're like two evenly matched fencers or chess players. Your implants and prosthetes are about as good as mine, but you're gaining on me every hour. I have the slight advantage of age and guile and force-screen reserves. But shit—I have to be a one-punch nightclub fighter to survive. The strength is all yours . . . or will be very soon. Come on, we can all have a few more kicks together. Or apart. I don't much give a genuine damn any more."

Jonas crosses his legs and gives Jason a distant, appraising look. "And, is there really no alternative to our little familial unit having to stay billeted together?"

"No truly practicable one, no. You could subsist for awhile as a nomad, but your source of organismic nurturance is in this very housing unit—this billet piston. You have to stay plugged in, so to say, for the re-charging and differentiation of your life-support systems."

Jonas seems to wax smug. "Carol and I got recharged very nicely in the sunlight the other day."

"That was strictly back-up systems absorption. Mild radiation effects. You will have to have intravenes and convection inserts and epithelial implants to develop at optimum rates. And you get all those goodies right here."

"Aren't you facilitating your own demise by being so informative?"

Jason steeples his hands and looks deceptively subordinate. He hovers over a long pause. "My dear boy," he begins, "there are simple deterministic factors operating here—factors all but inexorable, even fatalistic, unalterable. You will find that the social controls wrenched and forged into our system are so strong that we are held in check despite our best efforts to innovate. At the moment, you couldn't kill me, no matter what you did. Even with the truce code deactivated. And I couldn't kill you. Look around you—assume a passion motive. What could you do? How do you approach the task of killing me? My isomorphic field is permanent now. Getting weaker, yes, but you couldn't cut it with a phaser, or roast me with any thermal gadgetry, and do much effective impact focusing. Most of us unwilling putparents accept the short-term reality of death toward the end of our fifth decade, or when the offspring peak, at about six chronoyears, whichever comes first."

"If things are so pat," Jonas leans in, "so predictable —why is it that mutual hostility typifies the cohesive societal bond? Why can't we young have fun and be unguarded, and why can't the older people be left to mellow and die off happy?"

"Supply and demand of organismic power, probably. Planned obsolescence of parents, plus the glaring fact that the pool of energy is relatively fixed. There is simply not enough magnetism left to support familial groups."

"Not enough tits for all twelve Dachshunds, eh? So two have to play the musical mammaries bit."

"A simple but adequately relevant analogy."

"So why do we fight? What does it accomplish?"

"I've thrashed this through many times, and I always end up with the same general theme: aggression is *operant, instrumental, activating*. Cooperation is *respondent, conditioned, terminating*. To be cooperative is to be acted on by others. This is an explicitly deferrent, subordinate act, which generates dissonant feedback in the deferree, if I may neologize briefly. Homeostasis is not fully or richly experienced until hostile acts are undertaken. Hostile acts are somehow enervating and I think they are evolutionarily adaptive. Deferrent acts are neutralizing, ritualistic, mothballing, terminative. And you must also remember that hostility or aggression spans a very wide spectrum or continuum. We can be cutting in our speech or we can be cutting in our knife-fights. Now, come on, what do you say—shall we put on the Porsche and blow over to the gladpits?"

"Well, as you put it, we can't just sit here on our brooding asses. Hey Carol! Jason here wants us to go to the gladpits tonight—and go terrestrial in a sport-car reprod." Carol arches into a half-twist, the axis of the exercise cage aligns with her longitudinal thrust, and she spins out on to the deck. Ellen stirs, and sits up, looking vaguely exhumed. Carol jogs ever so slowly toward Jonas.

"We'll have to stay on pacific code to really do it right," she says, in bumpy rhythm with her jogs.

"Jason claims there's no room for the provobots."

"They can go on outriggers."

"Outriggers! On a Porsche? That's pure desecration! Besides, that would break up the flow of air and make a jewel look like a bug."

"Porsches look like bugs anyway," Ellen whines, "they're little. And funny-looking."

"A pathognomic dumshit comment," Carol bites the air. "I suggest you go on non-verbal, and hope for increments in your linguistic engrams."

"And for some esthetic sensitivity honing," Jonas says, "your opinion is curiously predicated on a lack of knowledge."

"I know what I like," Ellen pouts.

"What, prithee pray tell us?" Carol sounds merciless.

"Pontiacs," Ellen sounds like she is admitting to a weakness.

"Wow," Carol shakes her head slowly, "well, you be a good little splittail, and maybe Jason will let you dial one." She waits briefly, as if something were passing over her. "Anyway," she turns to Jason and Jonas, "I think we can swing a cozy double-date without any big bad Hansel and Gretel productions. We can take the new semantic monitor along, so that we don't overly con each other, and we can exchange persona banks—that'll have the effect of making us necessary advocates of each other instead of protagonists."

"I don't want to go," Ellen limps on to an inflective line somewhere between pouting and whining.

"Oh come dear," Jason soothes, "it will be exciting and perfectly safe."

"I'm afraid. I'm afraid of the children."

"Of course you are, darling, and they are afraid of us. But the fear is not something to stay with us all the time. We can be entertained with no real defensible reason for fear. Come. What do you say."

"Yes, little mommy-poo," Jonas sidles up to Ellen and touches her arm, as if testing for wet paint, "you'll have fun, and we'll all be on our good behaviors."

"Let's go on and get the car," Jason starts for the drop. Jonas responds immediately, then does a very slow double-take.

"What's your hurry?" he sounds almost baiting.

"No hurry. It's almost half to solar vertical. We can requisition the car, whip it back here, then blast off for the pits about half before sunset."

"No trick?"

"Keep it neutral," Carol cuts in. "It's obvious that you two should drift toward a peer-level relationship, and cut this dumshit emotional umbilicus."

"The stupidity of the blood-tie," Jonas murmurs, as if hearing the words from afar, "the unique accident of birth. My almighty, supra-personal, very own genetic self. And you—good old super-stud Jason! You—my very own putative sire! good old put-pop! Mounter of snowy female hillocks! The man who spiced and corned me—and I am supposed to kill you. And you me. Shit.

There is an overly neat, pat irony here. I sprout from your stalk and then turn my thorns back into it. . . ."

Jason pauses at the lip of the drop-shaft. "Ready to cancel the pacific code? Let's get on with it." He looks like Jonas's barbs are bothering him.

Young, small Jonas gets approbation vectors from the three people. The summated volition keys the deactivation of the spongy gelatinous force-field. Carol spins in liberated pirouettes, relishing the increased g forces. "I absolutely think I could fly!" she throws out her voice, as if ringing a post with a hoop.

"Amuse yourself, girls." Jason places a clumsy hand on Jonas's shoulder, as they lower into the shaft. Jonas looks half smug and half acutely aware of himself, like a sensitive, asthenic boy in a sweaty room full of gladiators.

The soft hiss of the drop-shaft dies away and the girls sit silently on the deck. Almost casually, Carol springs at Ellen, a wolverine at a poodle, talons arched like scythes, her voice grating the air like a banshee. Ellen peels off a little cry and rolls into the fetal curl again, twisting her throat away from the talons. The provobots activate, and Carol feels Ellen's isomorph, like a tough, pliable, plastic wrapper.

"Just want to keep you honest," Carol's voice is a strange loud coo. "I got the drop on you easily, and I can do it regularly. Just give me a delicious chance," she traces a teasing talon-finger, "and I'll gut you—from snot to slot. I'll give you a set of bomb-bay doors with no hinges. Dump all the sausages right out on the deck in one slosh and slumpf. You dig my motives, little faded goddam mother?"

Ellen cringes in her envelope, like a fat white grub in a glad-bag. The central console bleeps a signal and a mask-face appears on the screen. "Your kind attention," the voice is oddly ventriloquistic, "leasing span of four provost robots assigned to this billet expires in one hour. Credit lines show expenditures at eighty-seven percent of limits. If sequential leasing is desired, please code in request for a new line of credit." The face hangs in the screen like a mask on a spear, waiting.

"Code the rubber-plastic hulks out!" Carol snaps at Ellen.

"I . . . I don't know what to do," Ellen's voice is a soft crooning.

"I do!" Carol sounds almost comforting, as if assuring a child that you may indeed have any balloon you want. "You know you can't afford these big-ass bodyguards. You'll have to let them go back. In fact, I believe that Jason has just left you vulnerable. You can't authorize goods and services extensions, can you—you don't have the smarts. And hey, I don't know this for a fact, but I bet you don't rank as an independent social agent. You're a fucking conjugal ward, right? A little petal-skinned concubine, with all your brains between your legs." Ellen looks obliterated.

The voice from the visoscreen has a count-down anticipatory flow: "respond within thirty seconds or services will be terminated." One of Ellen's eyes oozes a fat oily tear. Carol hovers over her, fresh canine implants exposed. "Yeah, chuck the big dumb provos!" she barks at the screen, "who needs 'em?" The screen fades. The physiog plates of the provobots seem to lose tonus, their thoracic ports fade to a dull orange, and the sets of prehensile prosthetes retract. Like Zombies, the bots levitate slowly to the drop-shaft and lower into it. "You and me, baby," Carol rubs her palms together and looks at Ellen almost hungrily. "You and me. . . ."

IX

"Loosen up, man," Jason nudges Jonas across the mid-seat console of the terracar, "you're as tight as a spring." The car skims through the pressure tube like a projectile in a never-ending rifle barrel. Jonas punches the holovision and two players pump and wrench at the claviers of musico-synthesizers. Flowing spumes of color waft up in symmetrical Mozartian fountains. "Of course I'm tight. I feel outright dissonant, what with split sets of feelings most of the time. I keep waiting for something to happen—like when a bristling amphet blats in my arm and all the decisions zap out like Gatling Gun bursts."

"It comes and goes, little son," Jason cuts a vague knowing look at Jonas. The car blasts on to an open trench, stretching across a chalk-white desert. The effect is like riding into a surrealistic vista painting. Bruise-colored clouds writhe on the table-top horizon and the car's tach begins an unwavering climb, its dim scream levelling at 50,000 rpm. Jason punches new egress codes and leans back.

"Should be there in ten minutes, and maybe take an hour to get back."

"Can I drive it?"

"If you can do synch-shifts and free-steering."

"I can't."

"It's easy. Maybe I'll show you how. You have to *drive* a Porsche, or it will sure as hell drive you." Parallel trenches flick off on both sides, two, three, ten, thirty, and the car slows into a huge routing station. It is like swimming in an olympic pool with 100 lanes. The turbine whine falls away like a discus frisbee in a long trajectory, and the car clacks into a receptacle.

"The Ralph Nader monument is near here," Jason says, irising the overhead ports and standing up.

"I don't have any references on the name," Jonas climbs out on to the grimy ramp, as a creaking service bot rolls up to them.

Jason snaps the manifest plate into the bot's equator-rim slot. "A twentieth century Kee-Hoe-Tee—I never know whether to say Kwix-otic or Kee-Hotic—anyway, the guy who tipped the great money slide of 1980. The monument is a sloppy pyramid made of gold bullion."

The bot clacks out a new manifest route-plate, and the two figures, the 40 year-old and the 6 year-old, walk into the shallow geodesic station building. Escalators, pedwalks, airshafts, and turntables fill the air in cubistic labyrinths. People spin, turn, rise, drop, and scud along, radiating out, above, below, and around the station—a fat dowager with a liver-colored mastiff, bound for Steubenville; a regional gladiator champion and his entourage of flunkies, rising to the satellite deck; a cryonics salesman; a brace of psychographists; a chattering bevy of persona-swapping docents; fifty dray-humanoids for the Manhattan rock-piles; a vee-shaped wedge of half-scale quasi-homos, for interface servicing in Bayonne. The air smells of stale sweat, cold deepfat fryers, popcorn, acrid electric smoke, carnival smells. Asepsis kleiglights bloom on overhead and the air takes on a dryer, baked aura.

Jason and Jonas follow a color-coded pedwalk maze to a squirrel-cage shaft, then up onto a flitter deck. They notch themselves into the airmesh bunks and wait for the other seats to fill. The flitter groans into lift-off, hovers steadily, then soars off in a long shallow arc toward a plateau about one mile away. The gaseous energoid form in the seat across from Jonas makes him feel queasy, its nucleus pulsating in slow-motion jelly undulations. He has yet to see many of the life-forms allowed within the Synod's societal structure.

The flitter bends into a long approach shot and scrapes to a silicon-lubricated, skidding halt. A city reprod spreads out before them, blank, high dominoes of glass next to stone and metal gingerbread buildings. They take yet another pedwalk to a vehicle storage building and, at last, are led to the Porsche reprod. A ribbed silver fish, an aloof metal teardrop, a wing-tank pod with wheels, a fetishistic boliste, an apotheosis of terrestrial locomotion.

"What do you think of it?" Jason sounds proud.

"Snicker-snacks, pretty-pretty," Jonas responds, impressed, and trying to plumb the reasons for his feelings. He walks around the car, his eyes in pleasing transactional interplay with the black and silver surfaces.

"It looks alive," he murmurs, "pure functional esthetics."

"And that's no contradiction in terms," Jason's voice has an eager glint, "the car is esthetically optimal as well as thoroughly functional. Old Doctor Porsche was perhaps one-hundred years ahead of his time."

"I just got an informational reference blip that Porsche did a one-hundred and eighty ton flop called Maus."

"A tank that Hitler wanted. He pouted and screamed for it. Porsche humored him and tried not to smirk when the damn thing broke through the crust of everything except supracrete."

Jonas opens the door and slides in low under the wheel. He cannot see over the wheel and his legs are too short to reach the floor pedals. He stands up to get into the passenger seat as Jason bends his tall frame into the driver's seat. The effect is like peering through a slit in the cowl of a pillbox or through the fragile windscreen of a metal aircraft. Jonas buckles himself into the webbed belts and sinks back into the corduroy and leather seats. Jason turns the tiny key and the rear engine crackles into life, setting the air alive with delicious whirs and clacks and spinning, meshing, oily friction noises. He blats the throttle and the twin cams spin. The eight intake valves drink in precise goblets of fuel, the valves snap shut like heavy rivets in chrome walls, and the aluminum pistons flash up like ramrods, compressing the mixture of air and fuel in a ten-to-one ratio. A bright surging fleck of fire vaults the gaps of the four spark plugs and the mixture detonates, the engine turning restlessly at 1200 rpm. Jonas sits, fascinated and uneasy. He has never been in an internal combuster.

Jason moves the short gear lever into the top left quad of the H-gated shift pattern and eases the car out past a stiffly motioning Android. The route manifest carries them through settings of ecological splendor preserved by the Sociologic Nostalgia Synod: flat white ribbons of concrete bordered by live oaks and synthetic cypresses spin out to misty horizons. Five-hundred yards to starboard, groves of orange trees march in beaded rows across the breasts of soft hills, and fields of sugar cane rustle their stalks in the rich humid air. Reprods of ancient plantation houses appear as if in hazy dreams, pulsating poetic visions, the magic and enigma of old houses, mysteriously moving qualities, subtly insiduous loveliness.

"Plantation culture of the lower Mississippi Valley," Jason says, "with some incongruities planted in spots, like those orange groves." Small Jonas's receptor banks flood and surge with the mass of new inputs: organic architecture in ponderously scaled buildings, levees, spillways, weirs, bayous. The houses have a kind of vigorous architectural efflorescence. Plank roads appear, squishing into black, rockless alluvial mud and leading back into the thick wet woods where the oil-drilling platforms and natural gas wells stand.

A skittering mass of crayfish engulfs the road ahead in a two-foot high migratory rush. The Porsche stops in a shallow nose-diving posture. The tumbling flow of red creatures expends itself, clicking like a million angry knitting needles, vanishing into the spongy-floored swampland. Jonas pops the clutch, chattering the engine to rev limits, and watching the blower kick up swirls of dust from the road.

Raised cottages are visible in the tree line, long-sloped roofs shingled with scrub pine slabs and guttered with cypress. Jonas starts as a dark form disappears behind one of the huge barrel-like cisterns.

"Anyone live around here?" he asks.

"Some down-unders, predators, fugitives," Jason sounds like he is naming ice-cream flavors.

"Lions, tigers, and bears," Jonas quips, "munchkins, castles, flying ogres."

"The area has been under Synod control for longer than I can remember. Despite its appearance, it is ersatz. It is lifeless, dry, fragile. The life is gone from most of it and the facades are in force-fields and tractor-beams. An Uncle Sam reprod, a massive plantation structure, lost some beams recently, and part of it collapsed like a puff-ball, all brittle exoskeleton and fine dust."

"Why does the Synod continue to maintain the area?"

"You know—the sociologic nostalgia bit. The old cultural history, cultural heritage ploy. And, in the words of a nuttily candorous friend of mine, all this gives the natives something pretty to look at."

"We are in fact driving in another time era," Jonas muses.

"Correct."

The car whistles into rolling hill country, then foothills, and over a moderate chain of craggily inhospitable peaks, taking the switchbacks and S-curves like a gyro riding a string.

"A long sequence of inputs is chaining together for me," Jonas sounds on the edge of a profundity. He is silent for several long seconds. Jason looks over and is impressed by the poised posture and head angle maintained by the small boy. "Man, in his weakness and locomotive inertness, first brandished a club, then a shield, then thoracic armor-vests. Then came the stupendous discovery of the wheel—the circle, the never-ending surface. In the press of his instinctual drive for autolocomotion, man fashioned a chariot around his loins and harnessed the snorting horses to transmit the power to him. Then the evolution of vehicles—the names are pouring into me along with the visual engrams—britskas, drays, gigs, hacks, landaus, sulkeys and tumbrels. Then the reciprocating piston engine—who could ever assess the impact of that! And the tenure of it! Unbelievable! It's a goddam shame I can't do the retinograph projecting yet. You should see this: a three-wheeled French gun-tractor from 1770, the 1885 Benz and the Daimler the next year. Here's a 1902 Panhard Levassor that displaced 13,700 cubic centimeters and an oh-six Rolls Royce that got 48 brake horse-power at twelve-hundred rpm."

Jonas closes his eyes and draws his knees up. His force-field isomorph feels like thermal underwear. He snuggles into a tight ball in intent meditation. Jason looks at him with vague glimmers of pride and listens as the data continue to reel out: "The Benz that did 135 mph in 1909! Nineteen-oh-fucking-nine, daddy-boo! This Carrera hybrid can't quite match that. Bentley, Jowett, Ansaldo, Duesenberg, Bergmann, Tatra, Wills St. Claire. In-line fours, sixes, eights, flathead vee-eights, twelves, sixteens. Chevrolet, Maybach, Bugatti, and the Sunbeam record car of 1927—looking just as aerodynamic as the Porsche record car of 1937. Lancia, Oakland, Isotta-Fraschini—a towering name—a paramount torpedo. Am I boring you? I can do this subvocally. The input is like standing under a waterfall."

"No," Jason says, seeming to want the moment to be all Jonas's. "In fact, spin out some more. I'm getting some good deja-vu inputs myself."

Jonas closes his eyes and waits quietly. "The girdle of metal now protected man less, and propelled him ever faster, and the heightened responsivity of the machines began to feed man vectors of indigenous locomotion. That is to say, man began to equate the response of the machine with his own organismic response, and the symbolic corollaries here grew highly significant. For example, the machine quickly developed physiognomy, a torso, and extremities. The driver ate food, digested it, and excreted it. Does that sound far-out? In a reasonably tight analogy, the machine ingested fuel, compressed and combusted it, and finally exhausted it. In short, the machine quickly became an extension of man himself."

"Right!" Jason crows, Eureka-like, "a Porsche is to *wear*! It is to don! It is a mantle!"

"And the spectacular, navel-high Bucciali from 1932!" Jonas crows back, "the supercharged 540 K's, the blowers screaming like bull sirens, the Horch, Jaguar, Lagonda. And the tiny scarab of a VW from as early as 1937. The Alfas, Masers, and the snarling bloodred Ferrari's."

"Right on! Swing!" Jason blooms out, "I see a crazy,

razor-edged Triumph from 1952. It looks like a half-sized Rolls Royce."

"Fuel injection, transistor-metered ignition, mini-computes for troubleshooting—and finally, finally, on to the Wankel! Willie Woo Dumshit Wankel! One rotor one, two rotor two, one for me and one for yoooo . . ." small Jonas sings in a blare of non-contextual inappropriateness, "three rotors, quads—no pistons, no valves, no tappets, no lifters, no projectiles being shot out of barrels and yanked back by connecting rods. Instead, the divine, religious spinny-pin-spinning of the rotors! The model of the universe! Centrifugal galactic spinning!" Jonas breaks off into silence, and the camaraderie and euphoria begin to fade.

"Some input chaining!" Jason says, "your absorption limens must be worlds better than mine were years ago. Are you still getting the tapings?"

"Affirmative," Jonas tells him. "I'm going to stick it out and get the whole cassette. It's whipping through now like lightning—in condensed accelerates—smooth bands of trivid-cube data . . . hey, there's the super-rare Pegaso, a hairy looking Cunningham coupe, a docile, wallowing Nash, packs of MG's, and those ugly-beautiful 2 CV's. Fiats—God, zillions of Fiats and Jap cars. Astons, the pinnacular 300SL, the big square lump of a Checker, the vulgar Cadillacs, the beautiful plastic Elites that gave off high frequency sympathetic tremors."

"A Butler Porsche is unreal," Jason says.

"One-off, and throw away the mold!" Jonas returns. The banter quality of the talk rings as dimly out of place, but both the putative father and the neo-predator son seem to relish it in quick snatches.

"Here's a 1962 Thunderbird," Jonas continues, seeming to want to vomit, "it looks like a duck dipping its nose underwater. And here are other things you wouldn't believe: A Brazilian Willys, three decades of Vettes, from the fifty year-old OV 6 to the 1987 steam turbine, the Opel hovercraft from the early years of the 21st century. Mazda, Hino, Siata, the GM skates and sleds and aviettes. Bankrupt Rolls-Royce, the fiber-belt driven Dutch DAF, and the string of XP-500's and Golden Rockets and Club de Mers."

"What do you see as the big breakthrough?" Jason asks, beginning to act like a reporter taking notes. Jonas waits and listens: "Steam, baby—fine, white, wispy, steamy, steam! Then, of course, magnetic reciprocity and anti-gravs of all sorts, molecular transporters, short-blip teleporters, and the lightspeed drive-systems."

"And now," Jason says detachedly, "we have access to sporadic time placements, all in the name of sociologic nostalgia. From crawling and walking, to running and riding and flying and teleporting, we have come full-circle . . . no where to go but deep space."

The two fall into depressed silence. After awhile, Jonas dials medial somnolence and winks off into a nap. Jason prods his force-field with a small hatchet and gets no yielding. He looks at Jonas's closed eyes, then raps at his mastoid with the hatchet. Again, no yielding. He checks the protecto-limens of his own force-field, and wishes for auto-pilot control. At about 1600 hours PM, Jason turns the car into the familiar garage ingress-tube.

Carol bounces onto the hood, startling Jason. His anger flares, then wilts to horror as Carol hunkers down to spread her bloody hands on the windshield. There is blood on her mouth and her eyes are bright around pin-point irises. "I have done the deed," she coos loudly. "I have zilched the motput. . . ."

X

Carol shows Jason Ellen's body, lying on a chaise, the face gray-white, the neck punched open by two small puckered holes.

"I summated a pretty good stunbolt," she says aside to small Jonas, "then did the vampire bit. It got messier than I thought and the blood is no big deal epicurean pinnacle, like so many cats claim it is. But I zilched her good and proper."

Jason looks helplessly at the body and slow torrents of memories pour through him. Jonas looks at the body briefly, then turns away, as if irritated. Carol slides her hand into his and tickles his palm. "We may be able to stunbolt Jason right now—on the spot," she says, softly urgent.

"Do it if you can," Jonas returns, vacantly.

"We'll have to do it together baby—summated we stand, individuated we draw a blank."

"I don't think I can."

"Try, baby."

"Let him have his moments of grief."

"We may be passing up a very ripe situation."

"There'll be others—and very soon too."

Jason remains standing, looking down at the body, his chin sinking, flaccid, onto his chest. Carol moves toward him, in stealthy, fluid paces. She drops lightly into a knife-fighter stance, and her arm arcs out thrusting. Her face contorts into a grimacing mask as a flash of fire crackles from her hand. Jason starts and falls clumsily on the chaise. His movements are aversive, as if falling on a hot surface, and he dislodges Ellen's body. He rolls to the deck, the body following, slumping across him like a sack of wet, seeping cement. Ellen's eyes stare, wall-eyed, at Jason. He chokes off a deep bass sob, then seems to muster a curious composure.

"Fair trial, Carol," he says, through quietly clenched teeth, "but you can't cut it yet." Carol is on him in a flash, her talons ripping at his face and neck, but the tips scruff over the force-field like arrester hooks on a stone deck, producing tiny flurries of sparks. Jason begins to laugh: snorting, reflexive sounds, animal-like. He bellows, somehow triumphant, and Ellen's body moves, the posture ludicrous. Jason gets to his feet, his tunic smudged with dark blood. Ellen's thoracic power implant is clenched in his glistening hand.

"This is going to make me twice as hard to kill, devil-bitch of the world," he intones, holding out the power-pak like a dead pet. "Now, you just get your precocious little ass off at a neat esthetic distance, so we can get this mess cleaned up."

"Well?" Carol says, turning to Jonas, who has been watching, as if from the dark wings of a great stage.

"I see your attempts as defensible and adaptive. My current kilovolt-ampere readings show insufficient loadings to have buttressed your stunbolt appreciably. I feel no emo-level remorse at the demise of the here-present putative maternal figure."

Carol's face twists, asymmetrically, her expression a mixture of pleasure and disbelief. "Christ, you sound like a robot," she says.

"He's in a linguistic canalization stage," Jason says, loudly, almost as if small Jonas had now become his ally.

"Is that right, baby?" Carol asks, touching Jonas's cheek.

His response is trance-like. "Affirmative. Extraneous

vectors are being shunted away. I am on a single track. Theses and antitheses are spilling through my cognitive processes in compressed accelerates."

"Well, let's see how good you are. What are we supposed to do now? Our happy little familial tryad, you know—what's with the corpus delecti?"

"Synod statute simply require cloture transmission for goods and services. Disposal of the body is at the discretion of the mate or the surviving family member. The extirpated thoracic pak is in the public domain. Parsimony dictates pneumatic sewage disposal."

"Wow!—like supra-Machiavellian!" Carol says, hugging Jonas.

Jason goes to a wall console and codes in Ellen's goods and services cloture. He sighs as he sees the coding reciprocate assign half the index strength to Jonas and half to Carol. He calls the children to code in their DNA serial numbers. Archival trivid cameras tape the transaction.

Two workbots roll Ellen's body onto a levitator pad and carry it away, looking very much like pall-bearers. A flicker of wistful sadness glimmers in Jason's eyes, then he spins away and strides to the food console. He dials a vodka and onion-sprout spansule, drinks it down very slowly and lets the empty cylinder fall to the deck. He looks at his abdominal wall, his knees, his feet, and his gaze moves across the floor to where Carol and Jonas stand, like Jack and Jill. Jason belches and tastes the onion. He walks to yet another wall cubicle, and places Ellen's thoracic pak into it for safekeeping, thumbprinting it shut. He turns and claps his hands together. "Well, what are you two kiddies gaping at? Your big daddy-boo promised to take you to the wrestling matches—the big bad gladpits. So brush your toofies and wash your faces—we're going to be late."

XI

Jason, Jonas and Carol walk through the smoke and din and smell of the Madison Square Garden reprod. In the ring, far off in the haze, two hairy anthropoids roll on the matting, biting and clawing at each other. It seems endlessly far off, and the hoarse shouts of the spectators blare out over the sizzling cymbal-like background noises. The shallow steps of the aisle are smooth and mottled with tobacco juice and sticky food stains. They finally sit about six rows from ringside, squeezed in small wooden seats. One of the apes bellows a distress cry as the other clamps its jaws decisively across the neck area. Like a serrated vise, the thick yellow teeth hold firmly. The squat, quasi-humanoid referee examines the hold, like a spelunker peering in a crevice. He pounds a fleshy hand on the mat and signals quarter. The two ape-like figures separate, stand, and are whisked up into the hazy darkness. Tired cheers admix with boos and little ripples of applause.

"This is tame stuff," Jason says, turning first to Jonas and then to Carol, "primate-level preliminaries—wait and see the real gut-level show later. A bear and bull, maybe tarantulas, and a big favorite is the mongoose and cobra."

Carol comes to life as a Negroid mutant giant is pitted against two Orientals. The black hulk is heavily muscled, with webbed hands and feet, a prehensile tail, and a microcephalic head. The two Orientals have skin like yellowed parchment and their hands move like shuttles in a weaving device, their calloused heels seeking vulnerable spots. Chilling high vocal cries screech from the yellow throats, feet stomp in territorial displays, feints, stalkings, flinches, hissings. The pea-headed giant scoops up one small form, its robe falling away loosely, and scuds the mat with the body, upsetting the second man. He scuffles for a pinning posture as Carol screams "yellow bastards! yellow bastards!" One of the Orientals springs free and chops a hand deep in the groin of the giant. Both webbed hands fly to the spot and the giant gives a convincing display of resigned pain, falling with a concussive crash as both opponents hack away at his ankles. Then the small yellow men chop away at the back of the rib-cage. The giant whimpers for quarter as one gets past his testicles to prod deep into the unguinal socket. A buzzer erupts, causing Jonas to jump, and the three figures move up air-shafts.

A sonic cleaner fans across the ring and a Johnny Adatto holobot announces the next match: Amazons and midgets. Then two 300 lb. Sumos fight briefly and one falls back with a dislodged Adams Apple. A shapely young girl is matched with a satyr holobot, who finishes the pairing with a fierce, tearing, ripping intromission. His organ appears to have fins on its dorsal surface, the intromissive paradigm like a swordfish ramming soft coral clefts.

"Go! Go! Go!" Carol screams, standing, and thrusting her loins in copulative rhythm. Jonas feels translocated into the satyr's scaly hulk and feels the dorsal-finned shaft plunge again and again into the girl's moss-banked furrow. Deep at the base of his spinal cord, he feels a sharp vesicular twinge and his nostrils flare. He looks at Carol with a new appetite. In the ring, the satyr is astride the girl, like some bloat equine mutant, fallen obscenely on a snow white pillow. The crowd erupts in boos and hisses as the presentation ends and the pair of figures fade into the holodeck surface.

Two Samurai fighters stomp and clang their heavy swords together. Jonas winces in empathy as the heavy blade sings through an arm, severing the limb completely and notching into the rib-box. The arm drops on the deck like a Listerbag cut loose from its hanger. It twitches like a truncated snake. The brief empathy Jonas feels now flares into blood-lust, and he and Carol scream in high decibel stereo tones.

Dick the Eviscerator and the Danish Transvest Angel prove to be relatively tame, except for Dick binding the Angel to a turnbuckle and skewering him with barbed spikes.

"Good show, wasn't it?" Jonas says, settling into the rear-seat amniotic cocoon of the terracar.

"Blood and guts and screaming neurons," Carol replies, cutting a quick wink at Jonas. The two children slip into the control nodule of the car and lean back. Jason reaches between them to punch in the traffic code indices and leans back also. The car moves into a roundhouse and clacks into place. The deck plate revolves ponderously, clacks into a new position, and the car hisses into a commuter-trench.

Summated stunbolt, Carol vectors to Jonas, and he finds himself nodding and vectoring back: *affirmative—summated stunbolt.*

Jason dozes as the car skies through the trench. He grits his teeth and builds pressure in his middle ear passage. He strives for keen proprioceptive and somesthetic cues—flexing his implants, testing intraconnections, circuit breakers, sampling his powerpak reserves, estimating kilovolt amperes, muscle shear limits. *The little shits are sure to jump me anytime now, he thinks. They'll do a summated stunbolt. Maybe try to knock me off my feet, then pin me down with something. Or maybe they'll go for the head. With Ellen's thoracopak in me, they'll know not to try a breastplate shot.*

Carol's ideational engram implant picks up much of the thought train. *We'll hit him right in the jockstrap,* she muses. *Soon. The goodies are almost upon us—all the chattels and trinkets and options and controls of a centile 87 familial tryad. With me all cued in as consort, and counted as zilched by the census scanner. I think the first thing I'll do is take an all day sonic bath in a yogurt-tub. Then I'll wash my hair in ale and perfume and have a Cleopatra clone curry it a thousand strokes with a jewelled brush. Then I'll flux an orchid into my darling little pubes, and let little Jonas feel a catch in his throat, and some new itches in his epididymal wreathings.*

Then I'll have to find some garments lavish enough to warrant contact with my skin. I'll try those fine amoebic isos that cling to warm axillary grottoes, and send inflatable pseudopods into any or all my sweet little orifices. I'll just sit and dial all the sartorial cubes, and watch the models parade across the trivid-deck, and when I see something I like, I'll motion just ever so languidly, and the model will come and stand in front of me and she'll turn around slowly, acting flattered that I wanted her to stop. I won't have to say anything—I'll just make a detached little wave with my hand (the one holding the jade cigarette wand), and she'll know whether or not I have been pleased.

Then I may concentrate on doing absolutely nothing for several days, maybe even some weeks. I'll float around the house and canalize whatever inputs will keep my homeostasis readings quivering right at optimal—no readings within normal limits—none of the stock pediatric jazz about plus or minus one standard deviation. I'm going to get the pure input quintessence, the supra-

distillate, the clarified nectar. A quarter million metaphorical sperm may clamor around my slick organismic sphere, but only one gets to dip its little flagellate-propelled head into the custar epithelia.

I may vaporize all the surmats, sweep the environment clean, tabla fucking rasa, kick over all the arks of the covenant, and ram hot rods up the puckered assholes of every sacred cow I can find. And then I'll have a defloration ceremony that will make the coronation look like a girl scout meeting.

Young Jonas grasps the glowing lucoid control bars and watches the bank of instruments wink and bead into mazes as the terracar is tracked through the bleached gray foothills.

I feel a delicious burning inside, he thinks. *My skeletal frame is supple and resilient, like a young tree. I am neither jellied nor brittle, but flexible plastisteel. I can feel the bright strength arcing in my striates, like St. Elmo's fire on a drawn bowstring. I could plunge my hand into this instrument panel and rip out sparking conduits, and bits of walnut and leather and chrome, and throw them aside like a little bunch of dried flowers. I'd only flinch a tiny bit, but feel no pain. I'd feel a sensual pleasure—like crumpling a supercube made of tiny Danish matches, and having each shiny waxed match pop in a little explosion.*

My cardiac pump is so strong that I'll probably have to keep an autovector on it all the time—no hassle, but I'd have to have reinforced vessels to carry all that bright sticky stuff at top pressure. And I can feel my ramjet implant—it's like a private wind-tunnel. Inhale, and watch ten miles of Shenandoah Valley boom away underneath me! Set a coast to coast course, at tree-top altitude even, or shoot up to fifty thou any time I want. And my wiring! all the itching, deliquescing, neuronal snakes, all lashed and laced and tied through the skeletal frame, like glowing red pythons on the Effiel Tower. God, I feel oceanic—I am a king of the world.

"The king is dead. Long live the king," Jonas says aloud, and Carol stirs and smiles.

"And what sharp-edged pleasures are beginning to stire in the pit of my pelvic cradle. The anastomosing meshwork of duct—twenty feet of writhing ducts, packed into a bony nest. And twin horse chestnuts capped with tubing, and withering ejaculatory surges of 100 wrigglers per shot. And here I am, a little boy, accustomed to holding my little worm in my innocent hand to take a pee-pee. In the flaccid state, cylindrical. But, during erection, taking the shape of a triangular prism, pointing smack at my newly muscled abdominal wall. And, of course, smack at the furry little vaginal mouths, those pouting, puckered furnace-mouths, ringed with pubule foliage; the tender traps, the Venus fucking fly-traps, the window of the world, the uterine cosmos, the star-hole.

Carol snuggles against Jonas, and he feels his shaft begin to roll against his thigh, like a billy-club being placed gingerly on a thick lily-pad. In the rear seat, Jason sleeps, his mouth open, and his isomorph glowing a steely blue. Jonas and Carol turn to look at him, perhaps like parents would look in on a sleeping infant. Their eyes are luminescent.

"It won't be long now, baby," Carol says, slipping her hand under Jonas's toga-sheath. She spider-claws his stomach and pubic area, and feels the corded penile shaft. "That's my man," she says, "that's my big pony-stud."

XII

"Why don't you go take a walk ha-ha-ha?" Carol says to Jason, across the breakfast tray of zabaglione and papaya juice. Jonas looks up and seems to relish the baiting tone. The sunlight floods the room, emphasizing the textured excellence of the furnishings, the smooth resilience of the childrens' faces, and the palely splotted face of Jason, the putative father.

"Yeah, small daddy-poo," Jonas perks up, pointing a Bowie knife at Jason's nose, "why don't you leave us alone and go see some of your cheap geriatric asshole buddies?" Jason looks guarded and far more afraid than competitive. He tries to eat, but Carol keeps nudging his arm with a wickedly sharpened hawkbill cleaver.

"Can't let you two out of my sight—Carol, would you stop that, and let me eat?"

"I might, fat putfat shitface, and I might not—strictly depends on my beautiful feminine wiles." She draws the blade across Jason's hand and feels the iso give slightly, like an air-raft being stroked by a sharp stick.

"There's no need to be mean. What are you accomplishing?" Jason says, but he knows his question is hollow and meaningless.

"What do you think?" Jonas booms in, "your god damn *dee*-mize, your honored hour of absolute zilch, your hoarse, and maybe whimpering swan-song. Do you die well, Jason? I mean, like, pal of my cradle days, can you stand on the rim of the freshly dug trench, with the wet earth smell filling your nostrils? Can you stand without a blindfold and bellow FUEGO! at the firing squad? Or, can you sit at the banquet, say goodbye to your peers and students, and then call for the physician to come and slice your wrist under the table? Can you laugh at the electric chair? Or stop screaming when the napalm sticks to you like burning glue?"

"I'll die the best way I can," Jason replies, his voice somehow stronger. I'll take a terminal pill before I'll let these kids torture me, though, he thinks.

"How shall I kill thee?" Carol intones, striking a Thespian-Stentorian facade-pose, "come, let us count the ways——" Jonas claps and cheers. "We shall kill thee to the depth and breadth and height of our innovative souls' powers."

"Plagiarism! Author! Author!" Jonas roars, and Carol gives a demure bow.

"We will zilch you freely, as we strive for autonomy; purely, as we turn to the hedonistic rewards of adulthood. We will devitalize you in one awful, soaring sweep of passion, and with the griefs and faiths of our brief childhoods——"

"A morbid travesty," Jason says. "Carol, your putative father dived into the fire-troughs at gladiator school. I may just cheat you hangmen by wolfing down a big fuzzy terminal pill. What do you think of that, Miss Medea-Vixen?"

"Make a move to do that and you'll get stunbolted —hey, speaking of stunbolts, where the hell is that dawg-ugly surmat?"

"Sleeping on the pod again," Jonas says.

"Well, let's have a little fun with her."

"Leave her out of this," Jason says weakly, "she doesn't understand."

"She understands punitive motives," Jonas says, expectantly, sarcastically.

"And all about squelching funny-fun-fun spontaneity in us kiddy-boos," Carol says, leaving the table and walking slowly toward the charging pod, where the surmat dozes, like some incongrous Occidental Buddha.

"Off your ass, you ugly flaccid clod!" Carol taunts, kicking the shiny shins, and cutting off the charge-rate controls. The form stirs and looks up, like some dumb bovine animal. "Mawster Jason wants you to suv him some brondy."

"Horrible Alpha brat," the surmat mutters, standing up, and beginning her slow waddle-gait toward Jason. She sees the expression on his face and turns as Carol rams a stunbolt from the floor straight up through the burlap folds into the crotch. An animal cry of outrage breaks from the straight-line mouth, and the surmat scuds forward, like a disjointed Frankenstein. She falls over a ridge in the deck and sprawls flat. Jonas springs astride her in a flash, sitting on her neck and flicking stunbolt arcs onto her auditory flaps. Carol pins the heavy legs to the floor with a savage thrust and wrenching grasp of her taloned hands. "Freeze her!" she spits at Jonas, who opens his mouth like a dragon and ejects a spume of liquid nitrogen onto the squarish cross-stitched head. The surmat lies still, deflated like a beached whale.

Jason cowers in his iso as Jonas advances toward him, mouth open. Carol circles to one side, moving her hands like a beater in the jungle. Jason autovectors full-saturate autonomic fibrilation, and his hands fumble for the teleport bezel. He winks out of sight as Carol snarls in disappointment. Jason hangs about fifty feet above the billet-piston and feels himself sinking slowly, losing power. He settles on the promontorium deck, like a deep-sea diver touching bottom, his trembling hands grasping one of the trivid sensor masts.

"He's on the roof," Carol says, lifting her head, her

cochlear cilia stiff as thorns. "Like a tired old sea captain, waiting for his ship to sink," Jonas says, looking up and probing with his visual sensors. "I think the old stud is waxing tired."

"Does he have the extra thoracopak?"

"Yes, but he also has transplant troubles. The DNA webbings aren't holding the pak in place. The power flow is diffuse. In short, the old man's leaky."

"Is he vulnerable?"

"Does a hobby-horse have a wooden ass? Affirmative, both."

"Well then, let's do it. Did you dephase the surmat?"

"Yeah, the old granny-bitch is out like a light."

"How shall we do it?" Jonas asks, looking playfully dumb.

"Do you dig pure, rank sadism?"

"I *will,* I think."

"Well then, I say knock him off the roof and impale him on something symbolic—like a pikestaff——"

"Or maybe hang him on a meat-hook—by the armpit."

"Sam Duckhardt made a putfat hunker down on a bayonet till the point blipped through his belly-boo."

"Burning is always pinnacular. . . ."

The two children walk toward the airshaft, their gaits vaguely stealthy; but far more than stealth, a keen locomotor sureness is projected, and a sense of agility and physical power. They walk a little like killer-bots: a swiftly closing, homing-in, canalized pace-pattern. They enter the shaft and rise to the promontorium deck.

"Peek-a-boo!" Carol screams as the door hisses open and Jason spins to meet them.

"Hey—vivisection!" Jonas trumpets, "we forgot one of the better zilch-modes!"

Jason drops into a reflexive gun-fighter posture and backs away from the advancing children. Their bodies crackle in the luminescent iso-fields.

"Want to do anything ceremonial, old Dad?" small Jonas coos, moving obliquely toward Jason. Carol pads along the fair railing, her talons flicking in and out. Jason moves his tongue and feels the easy resilience of the terminal capsule between his molars. Floods of memory-traces stream through his ideation, rich cataracts of color and warmth and diapason sounds. "It's been fun, kids," he says, faint quavers nudging into his strong voice. He feels the organismic power flowing from him, like fluids filling fresh vacuums. Carol flicks a low bolt at him and he sags to the deck, his arms around another of the cold alloy masts. His body iso begins to fade to a thin exo-skeleton. Carol bends over him and flashes her long canines out over her lip line. Jonas mounts his knees, like a bareback rider, and looks hungrily at the peaceful physiog tones.

"Any last wish, big Jay?" Carol says, her voice hoarse and taunting, consummatory, ritualistic. She lowers her mouth onto his deltoid and bites, like a staple piercing a nectarine.

"No, baby," Jason whispers, his iso fading. He looks steadily at small Jonas and smiles. An aesthete satellite sings over the house, bathing the deck in warm diffusion and ethereal musico-vectors. Jason cathects the last re-serve of his fulcrum energy, and grabs both the small forms in his arms. He strains for a few seconds of raw strength, a final embrace, a dominant bear-hug.

"Live it up, kids," he whispers. Then bites into the pressurized capsule and swallows the fluid. The fibri-nolysins ionize the blood immediately, and Jason drops softly onto the deck plates. Carol bends to bite the jugular, then spits. "Ugh, he's all bile," she says, snapping her arms akimbo, "he did his own zilch, goddamit——"

"We can still defile the body," Jonas says.

"No, the archival cameras will be on us," Carol replies, looking around and pointing at a slowly telescoping shaft in the lid of the service core.

A camera pod atop the shaft revolves toward Jason's body and winks on. The mechovoice begins:

> ENERGY ALLOCATIONS FOR THIS DOMICILE REQUIRE RE-ASSIGNMENT. CODE IN GOODS AND SERVICES CLOTURE WITHIN ROUTINE TIME LIMITS. SUBMIT INVENTORY OF PROSTHETES AND IMPLANTS OF THE DECEDENT. CONGRATULATIONS ON YOUR NEW ADULT STATUS. ASSIGNMENTS WILL FOLLOW.

Carol and Jonas seem compliant enough, standing in front of the softly whirring camera. The lens goes dark and the arm lowers into the deck.

The new young adults return to the solarium area and code in the clotures. They dispatch two charbots to recover the body. They authorize autopsy, extirpation of implants, and vaporization. They sit on chaises and gaze at a fireplace reprod, looking deceptively like small children.

XIII

The vast Sea Island Complex spreads along the Georgiana coast for fifty miles, its geodecks, turrets, and monoliths reaching up into the rich humid air. In one of the honeymoon domes, Jonas and Carol sit on filmy discs, watching the trivids. Jonas drains a small flask of vodka extract and orange pulp and turns to Carol. "Happy, little one?"

"Ecstatic!"

"Come, award Jonas a huge kiss."

"Upper persuasion for lower invasion?"

"We haven't ravished each other for at least an hour."

"Let's do it on camera."

"And dig the holos?"

"Supra-affirm, Carol's juicy stud." Jonas kisses her, as if drinking from a spring, and Carol writhes and whimpers and makes urgent little noises in her throat. Her hands hold his face, both ears, and move to the neck; she squeezes the deltoids, skims her fingers down the latissimi, and holds both gluteal globes like honey-dew melons. Her fingers search inward, seeking out center-lines, symmetry points, downy hair patches, puckered sphincters. Jonas's small body begins to redden.

"Let's do a total eclipse," he says.

"Anything you want, baby."

They spring to the floor, like nymphs jumping from the tops of mushrooms. "Dial it the way you want, honey," Carol whispers to Jonas. He crosses the satiny deck and examines the life-systems console as Carol does a cotton-soft cartwheel and lies supine. Jonas adjusts some bezels and toggles, and steps back, as if anticipating the sound of a favorite disc or tape or cube. A low bolero beat begins and willowy pastel colors ease from the compositor nozzles. Jonas falls softly prone and reaches out for Carol, as if inching flat across thin ice. He grasps her hands. The two small honeymooners lie like trapeze performers, arms outstretched, head to head, spread-eagled, Carol supine, Jonas prone. He begins to move slowly, his head now softly butting against hers, then lifting to kiss her forehead, eyes, and mouth. He hovers over her face, studying the inverted lip-line, closing his mouth over the sweetly humid folds.

"We're forming a Yin and Yang bond," Carol whispers, her head turned to look at the trivid deck. Jonas looks to see himself bent over Carol, knees drawn up slightly, as if crouching to receive a per anum thrust. He lingers over her small breasts and feels her tongue circling his own hard nipples. He probes her navel with his tongue, as her darting tongue flicks deep into his umbilical roothole. He whimpers as Carol sucks his navel into a convex bud, then lets it snap back to deeply introversive concavity. Carol then feels Jonas's silky ramrod nudging at her head and his mouth trailing soft kisses down a plumb-line to her pubic thatch. As he settles there, she draws the swelling shaft deep into her mouth.

The compositor builds to plateaus of convoluted sound, smoothly writhing melody lines, insistent chordage beneath, and undergirding pedalpoint lines. An exquisite sense of imminence sharpens the crescendo, a sforzando clarion flares, and the children shudder together in a grand mal orgasm.

"Good God," Jonas sighs, breathless, "how often can we pull off these orgasm pinnacles?"

"Whee, baby," Carol says, her voice like a siren winding down, "about every two hours is par for us."

"The feeling is absolutely oceanic."

"The nicest thing that happens to us."

"And there are ways to hone the craft?"

"We've barely scratched the surface, baby."

"How does it feel to you?"

"Velour flags fluttering, the pelvic floor throbbing, velvet buzz-saws, hard jellied bats streaming out my rectal port——"

"Voila! an old man dragging a chain out of my ass——"

"With barnacles on every link!"

Carol turns thoughtful. She dabs at herself and stands. "Our lives should go far beyond hedonistic kicks" she says.

"That was overly self-reflective considering the spirit of the moment."

"I know, baby . . . I was just thinking of the assignments——"

"Assign—asshmine!" Jonas vaults up and dials a thundering buffalo stampede, "if we can keep from sprouting offspring, the years ahead will be a huge blast."

"We could get a fecundity assignment anytime depending on the population trends. . . ."

Jonas dials a Stearman Bipe and dives it low over the stampede. He hangs the craft in a steep stall and lets it drop onto the herd. There is a simulated crash and an impact reading.

"You're going to ruin the set," Carol says, an authoritarian edge capping her voice.

"It's programmed for anything we want" Jonas replies, "we could crash a fleet of 757's onto New York Megalop—say that's an idea!"

"No, baby, that's too——"

"Apocalyptic?"

"Shit, Jonas, planets have exploded, Novaroonies. One mothballed skyscrape nostalgia pit wouldn't matter——"

"You didn't have to be anal-expulsive."

"Sorry. I know what's happening. We should be sleeping now. Let's wink off until the absolute refractory phase gets past. Look at the readouts."

Jonas looks and starts. "God, is that us?" he asks, squinting his eyes at the life-systems screen. "Indigenous motivation at centile two? What the hell is wrong?"

"Ten orgasms in twelve hours, honey-boo."

"We're vulnerable to, well, extrinsic dangers, aren't we?"

"Yes, but not here. Not now. Sea Island is a kind of copulatorium magnatum. There's so many of us here for the same purpose, under the big protective Synod umbrella, that we're all but invincible. We can take most noxious stimuli and shunt them aside.

"This new sex regimen will wear us thin for awhile, but at the same time, our mtv's are getting fattened. If we got slingshot into deep space, we'd be happy enough with our memories. So sleep now. I have a special epicurean treat planned for tonight."

XIV

"Nuts, Sherry, garnished cold soup. Lobster crêpes, white wine, duck, Bordeaux, ginger sherbet, champagne. Lamb, salad, cheeses, croquembouche, cognac!" Jonas rolls lightly on a film-chaise, both his hands fondling his stomach. "Magnificent! the very top! You're a gustatory wonder!"

Carol lies on a chaise, stroking an ocelot. "Maybe you can begin to see why the rich think their shit don't stink," she giggles.

Jonas feels nudged out of context, but his satiety overrides all else for the time being. "Wherever did you find the menu?" he asks, undaunted. "Famous dinners of all time," she replies lightly, "same old jazz. Everything's in the console tapes, plus whatever we may want to innovate or random-match or compose. Gustatory Alps on Alps arise! There are gastronomic masterpieces aplenty."

"And we have access to them."

"Yes, my precious, assuming we stay assigned to this billet, we have access to a great many things."

"And I have access to you, my baby!" Jonas crows happily, leaning across the tiny table to kiss Carol's breast cleavage. Her eyes seem to harden and Jonas feels her faintly stiffening muscle tone.

"Accessibility is a two-way street," she says, "the extent to which we please each other can be a fragile proposition."

"Your response is aversive, and your verbal content implicitly negative."

"A bit of tough shit, Joanie." The color drains wanly from Jonas's face and he backs away from Carol slightly.

"I'm puzzled by your rather spiked response to my accessibility comment. And I'm not sure but I heard you say something like tough shit."

"You heard it right, little man."

"I am going to ask that you clarify yourself. Give me some sort of benchmark to show that you are basically conciliatory."

"Oh, you're such a little boy, Joanie——"

"Are you trying to piss me off . . . I mean, are you tampering with my responsivity for some reason?" Carol leans in close to Jonas, screws up her face, and sticks out her tongue. "Bleeaaah!" she imitates regurgitation.

Jonas's hands snap out for her throat, but his fingertips only graze her chin as she ducks away. Jonas feels adrenalin pour over his viscera like hot starch on a slab of liver. Carol rolls, like a paratrooper hitting the ground, but Jonas pins her quickly. "Monster!" she screams. "Rapist!" Jonas's knees nudge into her biceps, and her writhings slow to waxy flexibility. Jonas sees flares of ideation, in which he is flailing trip hammer blows into Carol's small face. He raises both his fists, then sees her face glowing with an epithelial luminescence, her mouth invitingly open, and in her eyes a pure message of feline receptivity. With a burst of reserve fulcrum power, she sits upright, tumbling Jonas softly onto her lap. "Now, come, let me kiss you, baby," Carol coos, lowering her face over his.

"You're an absolute tiger, Carol—God, you set off my rawest instincts!"

"That's a part of being supra-human, baby—we can inject excitements into each other without internal inhibition. We don't have to worry about psychological defense mechanisms. In fact . . . come, let's sit up in the crow's nest—we can read each other's sub-vocal engrams——"

"I know," Jonas cuts in playfully, "I've been probing yours for the last hour——"

"But I know! I know!" Carol sings. "Here, see if you can catch this. . . ."

Jonas tacks onto her train of memory-trace variables, following the convoluted pathways: semantic chainings at centile 99; reciprocal, self-cancelling diction paradigms; subtleties; inverted proverbs; then blarings of Id-level energy, rage, black sullenness, variable compassion, hormonal tropisms, sadism nesting in red pustules.

"Wow, pretty visual!" Jonas says, obviously impressed, "and with strong messages."

"It's not adaptive to probe very long at these levels, though," Carol says, snuggling against Jonas, and pointing at a borealis starburst low on the horizon. "The success of our pairing is not really fragile at all, it is assuredly probable. We should be very near our optimum developmental asymptotes. There is no emotional dependency, no infatuation, no personality adoration, no stiff Platonic love, no cyclical itching at the gonads—" A duck green flitter skims low over the crow's nest, bleeping routine attention codes. It banks shallowly and settles into a landing pattern, pointing for the recovery net below Jonas and Carol.

"They're our new neighbors," Carol says, "coming to visit."

"What are they like?" Jonas asks, opening the ingress netting and watching the filmy little craft settle into the niche.

"Anachronists, basically," Carol says. "Centile 50 throwbacks. But, tough on the stamina stanines, and tough in a kind of thick-skinned adaptibility."

"What sort of relationships are we programmed to have with them?"

"No hassle. The usual reciprocal buttressing of auto-worth parameters. It'll come easy as pie."

XV

Carol dials a Monaco skyline for the wall and neutral melody clusters on the compositor. She sits on a divan reprod beside Jonas and looks across at Dan and Lila, the neighbors. Dan is short and fat, with a face like a muffin, and Lila is generally asymmetric, but with 42 E-cup pneumobreasts and milky white skin.

The initial rapport aura is brittle, tentative, uncrystallized, and Dan can't seem to position his legs comfortably. Carol vectors in a wedge of camaraderie and the interactional matrix loosens. "I've been admirin your Porsche car, Jonas," Dan says, "are they as good as they claim?"

"More than," Jonas shortens the response, "but then, I'm neophyte-level with internal combust reprods."

"I'll stick to the stock flits and the public teleporters," Dan says, projecting both constriction and homey smugness.

"Face life in a Portia," Carol quips.

"I used to just love to watch the trivid nostalgia stories," Lila says in a high voice, "one of them was called *Portia Faces Life.*"

Carol stands and smooths her body iso into nicely flowing contour-lines, smothering a tiny giggle with a cough. "What would you like to injest?" she asks, walking casually through the heavy loops of rug-decking toward an ingestion console.

"What will you have, dear?" Dan turns to Lila.

"I just love Alexanders."

"And I'll have a Canadian Club and coke-extract," Dan adds.

"Tequila and bat-blood!" Jonas blares, turning to watch the neighbors modulate their winces.

"And a tiny little Absinthe and MDA for me!" Carol sings, pressing the control tablets and watching the panel lights blink and waver.

"Do you have, ah, children?" Jonas asks, holding his glass up to the kleigs, as if looking for worms.

"Goodness, yes," Lila beams in, "we have two lovely daughters, just no trouble at all, both about five years old now."

Dan tilts his glass up, his upper lip flaring slightly, and his little finger straightening. "I wonder if our kids are normal sometimes," he says, "ours still dig Ken and Barbi bots and making fece-balls."

"Dan, you shouldn't——" Lila seems embarrassed.

"No, it's perfectly allright," Carol says, cordially, "your pediat could fix that in a shake, I bet. Sounds like simple anal retentive fixation."

"Well, I must be on the edge of the inputs," Dan says, his tone both weary and testy, "I never heard of anal retention fixes, or whatever you said."

"Dan didn't get programmed for advanced cognitive awareness," Lila puts in, "but he's got plenty of common sense, and is just marvelous working with his hands——"

"What do you do . . . ah . . . what phase of working do they have you programmed for?" Jonas asks carefully, sticking his long tongue into his bright red drink, like a pseudopod. Dan watches the prehensile tongue interestedly.

"They've got me selling clothes over at the haberdashery reprod, and before that, it was flitter leasing——"

"And don't forget the death insurance stint," Lila says.

"Yeah." Dan turns to place his glass on a hassock, "can you imagine that? Me, trying to sell death insurance? But it only lasted six tiers. I'm at centile 50, and I guess sales is my bag of vocational goodies. What do you do?"

"We're newlyweds," Carol chirps, "I guess you could say we're still living on our putpars' estate and waiting for the fecundity schedules."

"I'm just beginning," Jonas says, "I do know that I'm topped off as extraversive, cultural-intellectual, and emphatic——"

"Humility, Joanie!" Carol chides, vectoring in a wink. "J.H. Christ, you sound superordinate."

"Well, good for him," Lila chimes, "I wish I were smart. May I ask how old you-all are?"

"Six and six," Carol replies, then quickly and authoritatively, "and how about you two?"

"Exactly double that," Dan sighs, a whisker of pride coming through weakly, "though we aren't in your class on the cognition index."

"What do you think about the current Synod Chief?" Jonas leans in to Dan, wanting to keep the talk light and non-threatening.

"That dumb prosthetic bastard?" Dan whines. "You know, some days I don't believe there's anybody at all up there in the Bayonne Puce House calling the Synod shots. And, what's more, I'm not sure anybody could."

"Onassis did it fairly well, don't you think?" Jonas says.

"He had loot and genealogy and a sodomic Grecian charisma," Lila perks in.

"Hey—well put!" Carol lifts her glass at Lila.

"Yeah, Lila done been to college," Dan smirks. "She's pretty clever with words."

"Wherever are you-all from?" Carol asks. "You sound like expatriates."

"You ain' no alien, is you?" Jonas feints a finger at Dan, smiling.

"Damn near," Dan says, with more seriousness than Jonas likes, "I got birthblatted onto a lucoid pneumomat in New Zealand, just before the genocide wars. Lila made it on an orbiting vehicle, and we met in Moline, at conjugation school——"

"Yeah," Lila says, "then we got caught smack in the middle of the population constriction, and found out vaguely that we had to produce some offspring, and that our kids would outgrow us and zilch us sooner or later."

"Jesus Aich Christ, how many tiers ago has that been?" Dan asks. "It still seems unreal. I mean, I slipped a cyanide pellet into my father's porridge, but it was on direct order from our pediat."

"The medical community helped to grease the works in the first difficult months of the parenticide phase," Carol puts in, "now the physicians are big absolute nothings——"

"Fucking ciphered witch doctors," Dan agrees.

"Capitalized on psychosomatics and random variations in remission rates," Jonas adds.

"And, all the while, our organismic reactions were precisely adaptive. Directly proportional to the severity of the impinging trauma," Carol says, draining her glass. "Anyone for more drinky-poo?"

"Ready, Rudy," Dan says, holding his glass up, like a student raising his hand.

"MDA makes me randy-dandy," Carol says, taking Dan's flask, and thocking his genital pod playfully. Jonas feels a tinge of something: jealousy, dismay, but then a sharp-edged curiosity and anticipation snaps into place. Lila leans forward.

"Do you-all want to do any fucking?" she asks, looking somehow lame. "I mean, like, we hardly know you, but you're new on the quad, and we want to be nice to you."

"And a change in semen is good for the girls," Dan laughs, looking questioningly at Carol.

"Fine with me," Carol says, her back to the three children. "How about you, brand new sweet stud of a husband-surrogate?"

Jonas autoprobes for cool emotional control, and finds himself accepting the group sex idea. "Lead on, friends," he says.

"I have a perfectly splendid idea," Lila says, "let's pair off and watch each other perform, say, on the podium. Then, we could try a trial and error quartet!"

"He-ing and she-ing, plus he-ing and he-ing, plus she-ing and she-ing!" Carol blares, handing Dan a new drink, and defluxing his genital pod. Dan stirs, a bit uneasy, and his pikestaff rolls slightly, like a soft bologna cylinder on a bed of wet leaves.

"Come, sit with Lila," Lila coos to Jonas, motioning to him, and motioning to her pubic thatch.

"You're just a real old experienced dog," Carol says teasingly to Dan, holding her small breasts to his mouth, "but you've been at it long enough to get stereotyped."

Lila has Jonas on her lap, masturbating him with deft strokes. "Ah, the pneumopillow of the world," Dan sighs, puckering his lips wetly around the jujube nipples, and nuzzling them with his eyes and ear openings.

"On stage! On stage!" Lila cries out, and Dan and Carol levitate onto the podium. "Do anything you like, you two," Lila calls, encouragingly, "entertain us—and make it good."

Dan and Carol do a quick tango, some simple yoked calisthenics, and frisk each other's bodies, squealing and tittering like mice. Carol lashes Dan's arms to an over-

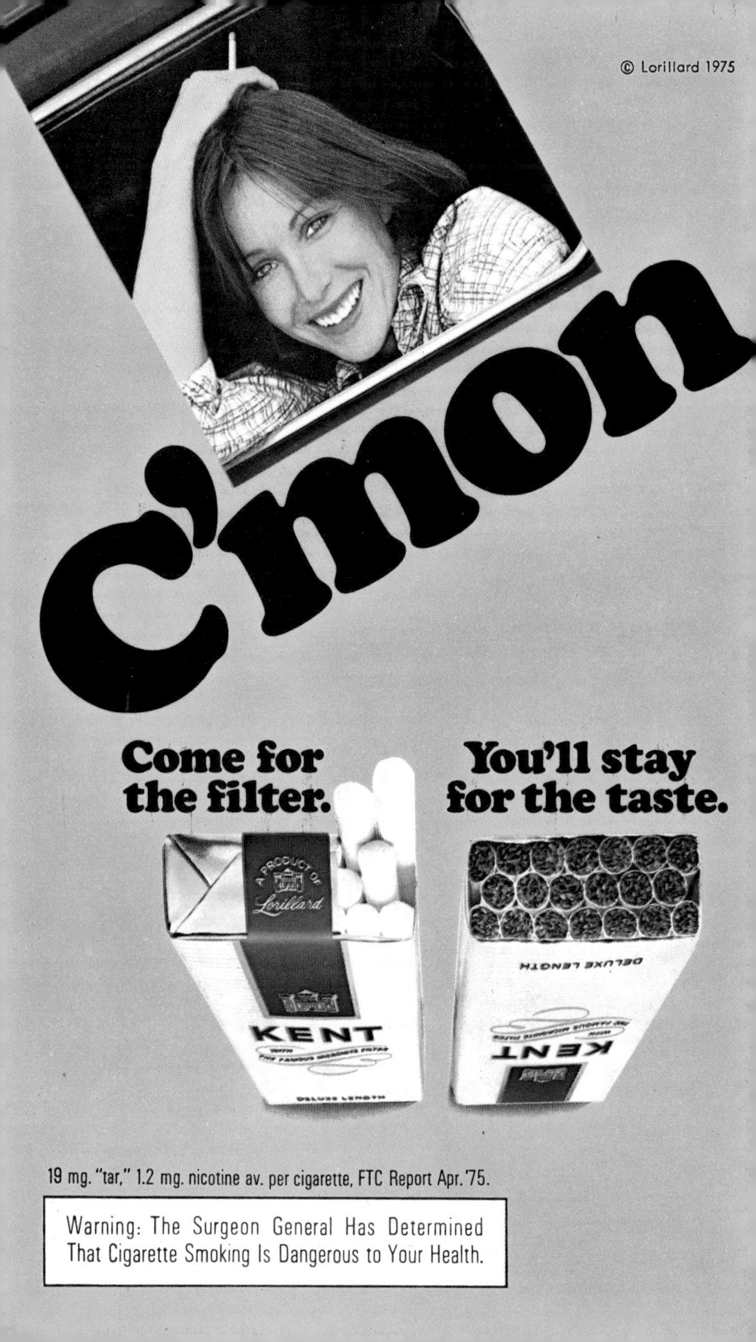

head bar and winches him taut until his toes flex to touch the deck. "Voila!" she cries, as she defluxes his toga-sheath, and steps quickly out of her iso. She moves over Dan like a monkey clinging to its mother, clucking, cooing, biting, squeezing. Dan's body begins to swell and his skin turns blotchy-red. He moans and sighs like wheezy bellows. "The coup! the coup!" Carol sings out, "watch closely, you love-birds."

She stands a few feet away from Dan and rises into the air. She draws her knees up tightly and lolls slightly backward, so that her genital cradle aligns with Dan's erect pikestaff. Dan bellows as she squishes onto him, like a sodden horizontal pile-driver. With her hands held casually behind her head, she tamps her body against him, heavily, squirming and thrusting in the graviton field. Dan's eyes wax to nystagmus, and he crows shrilly as his prostate wrenches and expectorates.

"Bravo! Bravura!" Jonas and Lila applaud. "Better than Christian martyrs! Bravisimo! Encore!"

Dan defluxes his bonds and rolls onto the soft deck. Carol squats on the bidet and irradiates herself, smoothing her hair with charming little sweeps of her hands.

"We're on, baby," Lila whispers to Jonas, who promply cants her hips over his, gains intromission, and carries her up to the podium. He stands erect and arches Lila backward, so that the great white breasts skew to both sides. He pumps furiously at ten strokes per second, vectoring in supra-tumescence and delayed prostate innervation. He adjusts the graviton matrix sensitively, releases Lila's pelvic ridge, and places his hands on her pendulous breasts. He gathers them like dough in his hands, then sprouts the gleaming chrome talons from his fingertips. Lila feels the ten limen-points of steel and winces luxuriously, the talons biting the skin ever so slightly, and the arms holding her like a vise. Autovectoring movement from his freely hinged pelvic girdle, Jonas piston-strokes the vaginal sheath and does a Tarzan cry as his vesicles shudder and explode.

He withdraws and melds his pod shut. Lila floats rigidly in the field, her hair spilling over the edges of the podium, like overhanging moss. Jonas places a talon right on the labial folds and feigns entry. Then the talons snap deep into his fingers as he probes Lila's rectal port with stylistic postillions and she whimpers in ecstasy.

"Well, that was very nice, all of you," Carol says, sipping a tiny glass of cognac. Dan is dozing on an orthopedic chaise, Jonas dials some intravene blatters, and Lila lounges next to Dan, her eyes on Jonas.

"The paroxysm's the thing," mumbles Dan.

"Where did he pick that up?" Carol asks Lila.

"He quotes it endlessly. It's from some old DeSade cubes."

"Surely there is something beyond orgasm," Jonas says, and immediately realizes the dampening effect of his sentence. "But," he puts in, "if we apply the ordinary criterion of perceptual clarity and drama, I suppose there is nothing any more asymptotic."

"It is the very nicest thing that happens to us," Lila says, lying back in her chaise.

"Affirm, doll baby," Dan mutters, still dozing.

"We really have to be going, you two," Lila says, dematerializing her chaise-netting and floating slowly upright. "Come on, you big fat bear," she says, nudging Dan and ionizing his chaise.

"Yeah, back to the domestic bliss context," Dan sighs, "well, it's been fun, you-all. We must try it again soon."

The sky glitters with cold bright stars as the two 12 year-olds and the two six year-olds walk across the solarium deck to the drop-shaft. The furniture reprods retract into the environdial walls, the lights shimmer and dim, and the charbot stands silently, like a leaden sphinx. Along the quiet street, the billet-pistons hum their 60 cycle pedal-points, the asepsis satellites scud across the sky, and municipal flares brighten scattered pockets of the view.

"What kind of seasonal clime do we get for tomorrow?" Dan asks, adjusting his olfactory filters and looking at the muddled horizons.

"Early morning volcanoes," Carol throws in, tittering, "seriously, I liked the polar ice-air they pumped in recently. The millieu was so pure it fooled most peoples' filters."

"I used my trachea-tube two consecutive tiers recently." The milieu was so pure it fooled most peoples' the particulates keep increasing."

"Everybody talks about the weather," Jonas says.

"Zilchood, energy allotments, child raising," Lila sighs, "everybody has the same troubles. Goodnight, new friends." They drop into the flitter and into the darkness.

"Pretty predictable people," Jonas says.

"They'll never know what hit them," Carol says, "fiftieth centiles are fodder."

XVI

Jonas sleeps erect on a charging pod, like a wasp folded in its birthing cylinder. The headset and torso leads writhe slightly with the surge-flow of organismic energy: informational references, practical-social judgement, syntactics-actuaries, abstract reasoning, linguistic models, storage and retrieval cue-codings. An occipital cap feeds in visual attention engrams, visual comprehension, sequencing, synthesizing, encoding, decoding.

Jonas stirs as the somnolent pods ease away from his temples and he looks around the room. Carol lies prone on a pile of furs, the ocelot stretched luxuriously on her back. Jonas steps from the pod and smiles at the sleeping girl and her pet. The billet is quiet and Jonas strains for the sounds beneath the silence: the sighing of the ozone blower, the clicking of relays, the muffled clatter of the console tapes and cubes. Carol breathes softly, sweetly, and the ocelot gives off a deep contented chortle.

Jonas looks up as a charbot begins to move from a wall niche to an egress-port, beginning the anti-meridian security check. "Everyhing all right, Nellie?" he asks the charbot softly.

"Nothing significant, sir," the bot replies, "my sensors are picking up some mass in the rear corral—wait, yes, it's a flitter, and some vandal detritus. Nothing out of the ordinary."

"Wild teenage nomads," Jonas mutters, "quasi-humanos, tenth centile drones."

He starts to walk across the room, but stops, smiling again at Carol's sleeping form, and levitates silently to the promontorium window ports. He palms a switch and the opaque epi-shield fades. Jonas looks out over the megalopic vista. The needle-spires and beaded monoliths of the city-reprod stand dimly against the pale lemon sky and swarms of flitters begin to spiral out of the geo-decks, like bats from a cave. The structures etch stronger against the sky as a maize-colored lumino-satellite breaches the horizon, like a balloon bobbing up behind a table. Sooty particulate stratum lift, like cloud layers, higher and higher above the skyline, as the scavenger satellites activate their vacuum beams. Connector trenches and pedwalks stream out from the horizon in radiate-spokes, like a wheel ten miles in radius. The streets are still empty, except for some provobot sleds and sweeper vans. "Looks like a fair enough tier," Jonas says softly, and a cheerful cluster of notes and forms bloom out from the compositor.

"Another calendrical tier," Carol says sleepily, rolling the ocelot onto the deck and stretching, "did you sleep well, darling?"

"Fine as silk, on the pod," Jonas says, "what do we have to do today?"

"I forget. The curriculum's gotten so diversified in the last two tiers that I lose track of it. Spin the dials, my stallion, and see what the Synod wants of us today—and speaking of stallions, you seemed to enjoy pumping yourself into Lila last night. I never saw such an erectile pile-driver in all my six years."

"A new tumescent implant—it just came to me. And none too soon. What's her name, Lila, was a bit well-reamed and sowish."

"Well, it didn't seem to bother you."

"You weren't exactly a piker with fat Danny-boo."

"Heavens, this is beginning to smack of jealousy. Sex with anybody and everybody is an important civil right. Let's not talk about it anymore."

"I did get some jealousy engrams last night. I saw Dan as a copulatory master who might just please you mightily."

"Posh, baby—it was just a game. Just a social play, a mutual admiration group, a sharing of apertures and protuberances. Let's eat and talk and dial the trivid-news—we may have to do some sort of assignment today, you know."

"How about a communal bowl of hot gruel?" Jonas asks, posing his finger over a key.

"Thank you, dear, how charmingly 12th century of you," Carol replies.

The two children eat the rich gruel-pudding and watch the trivid news: Synod Chief John Kennedy, re-elected for his 27th term, is having spinal troubles again. After being exhumed and cloned in ancient times, he wears out readily. "God, I love that charismabot," Carol breathes. The energy crisis is easing, the trivid voice continues, gravity engrams are being drawn from Dakotan geologic cores. Mojave Desert fruit-grid farmers are retarding growth inputs of nectarinos until the Synod agrees to allocate more barter-energy to them.

"What the hell is a nectarino, Carol?" Jonas says. "Here, I'll dial you one," she perks, keying in a code. "Hey, a slick peach—and with pressure pods, too—funny-fun to bite."

The planet's bothersome tendency to skew and wobble orbitally has been lessened by re-cathecting magnetic lacuna near the lower polar undercap. And a wedge of desert heat will be tried in Maine. Zilch quotas are lagging in the Northeast Quad, normal in most continental areas, and ahead of schedule in the South.

A Barbara Walters holobot materializes for the nostalgia-bank station break. She does an Alpo commercial, and the West Highland Terrier refuses to eat the 76%

moisture pile of detritus. Barbara breaks up in laughter, her pre-dental lisp and heavy upper lip notwithstanding. A Mardi Gras holoprod is scheduled in the old city, and the Dresden firestorms are showing at the Megadome Cinema.

Jonas finishes his gruel and codes in the assignment index. Two cassettes eject, one colored Wedgewood Blue, and the other Ferrari Red.

"Sex differences," Carol says. "We're still anachronistic, after how many thousands of dumbass male chauvinistic years."

"The pole and the hole," Jonas says, with affected solemnity. "Anatomy is destiny—blue for a boy, pink for a girl."

"The object lesson in dismantling that myth lies in *me* sodomizing *you,* baby——"

"Not during breakfast, my ptarmigan."

"You'd feel differently, if you didn't have a candlestick hanging between your legs."

"Ancient penis envy," Jonas says vacantly, handing Carol the red cassette, and bowing in a flourish. "You might dial, say, Karen Horney or Margaret Mead, and get some input-saturates."

Carol smiles, unperturbed, and snaps the cassette into her forearm. Her face lights up as the message vectors in.

"Guess what I'm going to do today, honey-boo?" she asks.

"I haven't the foggiest notion," he replies, "but I'm slated to go to the Barter Complex and watch economic chaining theories—or something like that."

"How quaintly masculine," Carol says, "I myself am docketed for Geisha School——"

"Geisha School!" Jonas crows, "a monument to the distinctiveness of womanhood. . . ."

The compositor groans and emits the basalt-colored monolith-shapes of the vocational tier-phase. The geodome irises and the sunlight flares in, resolving into a deep yellow aura, gilding the children with gold-leaf burnishments.

"See you at lunch, maybe," Jonas says, touching Carol's shoulder. "Have fun at the Geisha thing."

"You too, sweetheart—and leave the puce flitter for me, please."

"Your wish is my command, precious flower." He walks to the egress port, slapping the charbot on its pneumoflex rump as he passes. Jonas notches himself into the flit and clips the cassette in the traffic code console. The little craft lifts, feather-like, its anti-gravs spinning in silicon matrices, and planes off over the billets, scattering a leathery covey of half-size pterodacts, out for a morning's soaring.

The helio-suns seem to fizzle and sputter as sulphur-colored cloud-balls scud by. Jonas drinks in the environment as the flitter slips over the domes and spires. He sings a convoluted melodic spiral, whistling a trilling third below it. The craft banks up into a regional traffic band, slipping in among hundreds of flitters. The stream of tiny planes narrows and thickens, funneling into a municipal commuter-tube, like bees swarming into a port-hole. In the tube, the airspeed of the flitter-swarm synches in with the escalator-like movement of the cylinder, and the sense of motion eases to neutral.

Jonas turns to wink at a long-haired copulatress, sitting in a rosy-hued duo-flit, her sloth-like pet sitting beside her, very close.

The girl yawns and waves, and vectors in *Hi baby, where's your surmat*?

Jonas flushes and the girl giggles. He ellipses his visual agates and probes for the girl's cranial wattage codes.

The girl feels the probe and begins to squirm. *Your brain is between your legs,* Jonas vectors in to her, reading her 20th centile intellective parameters.

Come see me when you get bigger, the girl codes, and the sloth bares its fangs at Jonas. The girl opaques her visopod and Jonas sulks briefly.

He scans the instrument panel: terrestrial velocity equivalent 742 mph, impact neutralizers activated, graviton matrix at 3 g's, barometric pressure 50 inches, temperature 62° F, amperage clusters optimal, and leasing cloture normal. He spins the music dial and gets a Bach flute sonata, checks his somesthetes.

The flitters suddenly emerge, over a barren moor, at about 1000 feet altitude. The sense of motion returns slowly, then exhileratingly, as the azimuth-tracker lights up, and Jonas's flit falls away from the thinning stratum of crafts, peeling off. His tracker-beam angles down, and he hones in on it, like riding a rainbow. He dives through a negatively decelerating trajectory, the wind whistling past the tiny windpod. The desert below shows a random pattern of pock-marks, craters, and fissures. A mountain range appears on the horizon, a dusky, lavender mirage, and beyond it, more spires and monoliths. An omnibus flitter, filled with cheering ten year-olds, wings in beside Jonas. Above him, a delta flit dips its stabs, and below, a geriatric honoree jockeys his Aeronca reprod toward the megalop. Jonas cranes his neck over the side as the flitter enters the city.

The spires are taller than any he has seen, perhaps a full mile in height, corkscrew-shaped, luminous, and marvelously well detailed. The monoliths are thick and massive, and difficult to relegate to the perceptual mundanity of binocular cues. Jonas has trouble fixing such huge masses in visual perspective. He rides the tractor-beam cone into one of the monoliths, and it is like a gnat flying at a skyscraper. The flit settles into a niche and is drawn into a cubicle. The pressure hisses and a port irises.

Jonas steps into an amphitheater and is met by a charming hostess-robot. "Welcome," the bot says, bowing, and motioning him to a seat. The room is filling with different kinds of people: humanoids, anthropoids, delicate looking pygmies, and some are rare gaseous energoids. Jonas sits between a pale adult woman and a leathery-skinned Sumo gladiator.

The lights dim and a Synod Elder begins to speak. The voice is clear and resonant, and Jonas feels the vocal timbre in his ears, head and even in his ribcage. He ingests the voice like food, like streams of deja-vu pictures and sights and sounds. It is the consummate voice of wisdom. With compressed diction chainings and the purest semantic distillates, the Elder traces the evolution of the planet, each sentence chain cleanly incremental, precisely relevant, routinely cogent, building toward a crystalline exponential point, the white-hot arrowhead of mans' knowledge, cleaving into the future darkness. Huge trivid decks bloom with scenes of the past: the colorful, innocent wars fought with grapeshot and muskets; the olive drab wars, with fearful aircraft dropping explosives; the nuclear, hydrogen, and cobalt wars, and the defoliation plagues. Then, the ignition of the planet's atmosphere, the world-wide thunderclap, and the orbital swerving. The Elder's voice drones on, like informational life-amperage to Jonas. It traces the underground years, the people grovelling for pockets of oxygen and fungi beneath the seared crust, the landings by galactic nomads, and the satellite armadas dispatched to fertilize the planet.

Jonas stirs in his chaise, the gladiator grunts, and the pale woman sighs. The Elder traces the foliage and compost decades, the hybridization of life-forms, the mutants and the recessives, and the organic cycles which yielded carbonized gems and metals. Then the obsolescence of supply and demand ratios, the extinction of the work ethic, the homogeneity of economic systems.

And now. "And now," the Elder's voice rises, "we find ourselves in life-settings much like those of our predecessors—alike in that we are destined to live for awhile on this planet, riding a spinning sphere through the ethers . . . and then, to die."

Jonas thinks back to Carol, her smooth face and ripe mouth, the hedonism of their life styles, and wonders why he has been assigned to a dreary evolutionary lecture. Almost in direct reply, the Elder explains the time-binding, cultural heritage concept, and the need for a select sample of peers to know the entire story—to have full-saturate experiential imprinting. Jonas feels a probe vector and turns to the Sumoglad, who smiles, revealing rows of squared incisors, behind slick, rubbery lips.

"You and me wattage peers," the Sumo grunts, and Jonas quickly reads the massive humanoid at centile 87. The man nods over Jonas's shoulder, and he turns to see the young woman smiling at him. "And I am your new peer also. Welcome."

Jonas turns again and the Elder's eyes are on him. He stands, as if commanded, and sees about a dozen other people stand. "Welcome, new peers," the Elder says, and Jonas feels the charismatic flood of approbation from the group, the rich vectors of warmth and empathy.

"There is an ancient saying," the pale woman says, embracing Jonas gently, "that a person may not have his cake and eat it too. You, me, all of us here, are exceptions to that. We have certain destinies, because we are cognitively superior—certain responsibilities, say.

But your life in your own home region is quite another matter. Do whatever you like, and you will find limitations entirely appropriate to your exploratory drives. You will come very close to living in the best of all possible worlds." The woman vectors in an autoworth flare that Jonas feels like a thoracic orgasm, and the Sumo claps a hand on his shoulder.

I am to be a Peer of the Realm, Jonas thinks, and the subvocal sweelings of accord ring through him.

"Yes, welcome, new, young peer. . . ."

XVII

"However did you get here so quickly?" Carol asks Jonas, berthing the puce flitter, and struggling with some cubes, "come, help me with these."

"You'll be pleased to know that I have a new implant," Jonas says, "and—*and,* it is a medium-range teleporter."

"How wonderful, darling," Carol replies, but a shimmer of something maladaptive comes through, like a little hurt.

"What's with the new cubes, and how did it go at the Geisha thing?"

"The monthly trivid gimcracks, you know, bigger and better hedonistic kicks. And the Geisha School was midway between a drag and a musty anthropologic excursion."

"I am to be a Peer of the Realm," Jonas says, with non-contextual playfulness.

"You are to be a goddam what?"

"A big fucking Realm-Peer!"

"Well, fuse my fissures, my own little Jonas," Carol cries, but her emoradiates register envy, and her facies read tic-like ambivalence. Jonas picks up the cues immediately.

"Aren't you pleased?" he asks, and her silence puzzles him.

"Pleasure derives from egocentric reinforcement, not from deferrence to superior organismic achievement. I would be pleased if *I* had a new teleport implant—especially a medium-range one——"

"Well, pardon the hell out of me——"

"Oh, don't start protesting innocence."

"I cannot do otherwise. But, the concept of innocence need not be introduced. I mean, what the hell has that to do with me? Or with anything at the moment?"

"I don't feel like talking to you."

"Your feelings are maladaptive."

"Who the fuck says so?"

"Well, first, your emosensors are flaring like hot irons, and the semantic monitor readings are far into the tail of the curve. In short, sweet Caroline, you are talking and acting and feeling like a dumb-ass split-tail bitch."

"Now, who's semantic monitor reading is piss-poor?" Carol says, feeling some indignation. "And what has being split-tail got to do with anything?"

"It's almost as if some important intellective insights are mediated by the dick. And you, of course, do not have a dick."

"I abhor appurtenances. I should mightily object to a spongy shaft growing in my pubic thatch. I have my very own sweet-scented cathedral entrance, thank you."

"It *is* very sweet," Jonas says, slipping is arm around Carol, "and I love it, and I love you." Carol's face quivers and she looks into Jonas's bright deep eyes.

"We've been quarreling again," she says, dropping her head on his chest, "I just can't be strong and adaptive every day. It's not natural."

"Be anything you can, baby," Jonas says quietly. "Be kittenish or be an unabashed tigress. Be strong or be dependent. Lean on me, or push me—but stay with me."

"I want to regress. At least for a little while," Carol begins to sob. "I want you to hold me," and Jonas folds her in his arms. "And I want to sleep for just a tiny while with you. Come, I want to sleep in the amniopod." They climb into a wall niche and lie in ventral-dorsal spoon postures. Jonas holds Carol gently, and codes in a short-primed coma-nap for her, and medial quiessence for him. "You'll feel better when you wake up," he coos to her as she drops into sleep.

He looks through the shield at the room, through the vesicle at the far end, and out at the horizon. He notches his vision to 20X and finds his magnification and X-ray abilities are far better than before. Voyeurism, he muses, as he zones in on fat Danny, watching the trivids, and little Mark Stitt trying to climb over his three year-old sister.

A routine check, Jonas rationalizes, and zooms in on neighborhood scenes. Gray Mall is asleep on a very hard pallet, her geriatric wheezings easy to minotor, and old Grace is dozing, her dental plates grinning at her from a bedside stand. Sue is picking at the patches of acne on her cheeks and chin and nose, and Dave is fighting with his provobot, as usual. Indian June is carping at her consort, and, deep in the sub-basement of his rococco reprod, Dr. Stevens is doing his vivisection experiments on children. Jonas steels himself as he zooms in on the scene, but the sight floods him with empathic revulsion. Carol stirs, and reaches for him, and he feels protective, holding the small form.

I'd like to carve that sadistic old bastard into cubes. But then Jonas thinks of his own eclectic feelings about sadism in general.

What a really fucked up society, he muses, *but typical, actuarially normal. People everywhere held together by reciprocal hostility and protective force-fields. Better take a shit in a bag, so you won't have to bare your ass over a commode with a municipal duct—somebody might just blast you off the seat. Keep your protective isos on, force-fields at all ingress-egress ports, flit in coded flight patterns, and watch out for geriatric roverpaks. Only in-*

side one's homeplace is there true safety, and this is only when there are no offspring around to mature in six tiers and start sizing you up for zilching.

My psychopathy index must be changing, Jonas thinks. *Perhaps being a Peer is going to change me. But then, they told me to do anything I wanted, and that the limitations would manifest themselves. . . .*

"Come, little one," he whispers to Carol, "wake up—we're going to a grand ball tonight."

The children stand in the sonic shower, holding hands, naked, except for genital pods. "Taking a bath used to be fun," Carol says, "I remember onyx tubs on raised dais, bubbles, steam, perfume——"

"Stretch a little," Jonas says, "I'll dial you some hedonistic salts that will surpass any tactile blast you've ever had." Jonas dials glycerol crystals and ambergris extract, and the sonic cone pouring down on the children is like butter and sand—light, clear oils, and billions of tiny cubes abrasing the ripe epithelium, skip-bombing the tender surface.

"Hey, the jet streams of the world are whistling right through me," Carol cries, stretching luxuriously.

"We are itchy neural sieves, baby—matter and anti-matter, prime tissue and hot myelin."

"It feels so good. So good."

"What are you going to wear to the ball?" Jonas asks.

"Whatever the time-warp suggests," Carol replies, airily, "or we can do the simultaneity bit, and flux off and on, depending on what the group does."

"I dig that," Jonas says, vaulting into a mirrorsphere and coding on some costume alternates. The mirrors revolve, changing angles, the trivid camera projecting Jonas's image from different angles and distances. The costumes change on autovector impulses: a riding habit, a zoot suit. "Hey, zoot suit with a reat pleat and a drape shape!"

Carol sits primly on a valve-stem chair and watches, amused, interested. A stiff sailor suit materializes, and Jonas pipes an air from Pinafore. A coarse-weave caftan follows, then a kimono, and a poncho; finally, a claw-hammer coat, cutaway and wing-collar, doublet, frock coat, monkey jacket. . . .

"Elegance, Jonas!" Carol applauds. "Try some elegance!"

Jonas codes in a Prince Albert, spiketail coat, swallow-tails and ruped dickey and flying wing.

"There!" Carol applauds again. "Hurrah for the sartorial tiger!"

Jonas watches the hosiery alternates flick through changes: anklets, boothose, knee socks, trunk hose, shears, diamonds, then spatterdashes, chaps, gambados. . . .

"Funny fun-fun!" Carol squeals, "let me try." She pops next to Jonas and codes some trials. "Looky-look!" she points. Costumes swirl onto her small body, then whisk off, replacing themselves, as if by magic: crinoline, farthingale, muu-muu, pannier, sarong, *chapeau bras,* Dutch cap, picture hat, sola topee. . . .

"Furs!" Jonas yells, coding a category, and Carol watches herself covered with sable, leopard, marten, chinchilla, tiger. Jonas dials a Parisian boulevard scene on the wall and snaps an absinthe blatter into his forearm.

"Forbidden nectar," Carol teases, rolling into a series of soft somersaults, luxuriating, hugging herself. "Where is this grand ball?"

"At a chateau reprod about halfway to the California fault," Jonas says, an excitatory edge in his voice, "a 60 room manor house, 28 ornate baths, basement, sub-basement, tunnels, catacombs, all 18th century nostalgiajazz, you'll love it."

The iso-chronon hums toward the dusk hour as the children cavort and tumble with each other. The trivid deck swarms with ballet dancers, the olfactory spumes smell heliotrope, and the audioports sift out symmetric sonatinas. Half a continent away, the huge chateau is glowing with hundreds of tapers in carved sconces, as the charbots ready the structure for the ball.

XVIII

"I met a tenured peer today," Jonas says, perkily, jockeying the flitter through the commuter flight-path, "who has—are you ready?—a global teleporter."

"Absolute zounds and incredulos!" Carol says, puffing on a Maduro stogie-pencil and watching a Watusi troupe on the panel trivid. "He must be at the asymptote of everything."

"An artist-physiognomist," Jonas replies, "and you're right. He is at three organismic standard deevs, and plusses past most ninety-ninth centiles."

"Rare. Unreal——"

"He pops to, say, Manhattan Slab, flits off to the Sears Obelisk, then—zap—maybe to Peking or Old London or Atlantis Megalop, to Everest or the Matterhorn."

"Do you know anybody with an interplanetary rig?"

"Just the bullshit artists at the blatterpub."

"What's your . . . uh . . . *our* new teleport range?" Carol asks, a whisker of tentativeness coming through.

"*Ours* is right," Jonas says, "and, I think it is about 2000 miles, or whatever the curvilinear equivalences are."

"Could we blast straight up, altitudinally?" Jonas's visual analogies crystallize, fade, synthesize. "Yes, little concubine, but that figures to about ten million feet. What would we do up there?"

"Enjoy the view. And fuck."

"Naughty, delicious child!" Jonas crows, planing the flitter into the continental corridor and leaning back. "It's about ten minutes to the teleport station, then a soaring, swooning blast to the party from there."

Beneath the corridor, the skimmers and transporters zip and flit in square, cross-hatched flight matrices, like hundreds of close-set reinforcing rods in seas of plasticrete. Vapor trails boom out from stacks and jets and ports, sucked up by the lumbering, rust-colored asepsis satellites. The flitter clips along the base of the corridor-funnel like a fat hornet scudding through a culvert.

"Almost there," Carol says, examining her luminescent fingernails, "I wonder what the girls will be wearing."

"Nudity is always stylish," Jonas answers, "and laminated things, like layers of flower petals." The flitter banks into the teleport station, a tall gray spire, the lattice niches filled with flits and skims and transporters. Just above the berth, a gnarled quasi-homo pouts in his flitseat, his thumbprint voucher rejected by Credit Control. Below, a black drone preens an UltraCauc Anglosax official, the powerful lampblack hands flowing over the hirsute form.

"Some really weird cats get issued teleport implants," Carol says, looking both ways, "pecking orders are so scrambled, so that you never know the players except by digging the scorecard."

"Can you probe the UltraCauc in the drabflit?"

"Affirm. He's a sixth-tier reincarn, stuffed with transplants and prosthetes. His goddam exoskeleton is soybean-based. I'm picking up almost nothing organic."

"And we, young tigers that we are, are organic from cover to core."

"Well, what do we have to do before the trip? vouchers? azimuth? release forms?"

"All done, baby. Coded and reciprocated. Want to hold hands? Or sit on me?"

"I used to be afraid of teleporting. I'm not anymore, but I still want to hold you." The children hold hands as the isochronon flicks through a countdown: seven, six, five. . . .

"Hold tight," Jonas says. "I always wonder if I'll feel the wind in my ears," Carol says, four, three, two, one. . . .

The children shimmer and fade quickly, and materialize in one soft pop 1500 miles away. They stand on a small dais in the entrance foyer of the huge chateau, a smoky cone of light falling around them. Jonas brushes his velvet lapels, a bit affectedly, sets a firmer jaw-line, and takes Carol by the arm, stepping onto the stone floor. Two eight year-olds appear on the dais, looking like plump mannikins. They blink into the lights and the darkness and step from the dais. Butler clones and housebots move about in life-simulation, bowing and smiling, carrying trays of blatters and fluid cannisters.

Jonas and Carol move through the receiving line, getting uniformly warm emovectors from the hosts, a tiny vivacious couple from Upper Montclair, the Mountbatten clones from England Volcano Slope, two sociometry programmers from Peoria Trench, and several beautiful Ava Gardner clones. Jonas realizes that the guests notice the Peer medallion on his forehead, glittering red and gold—their response is deferrent, smiling and ever so slight bows. Jonas and Carol move into a large central hall, high-ceilinged, vaulted, stressed with carved beams. A massive chandelier descends from the secret darkness, lighted tapers burning. The guests move gracefully, fluidly, around tables burgeoning with parfait derivatives and wines.

The guests vary in age and size and appearance, from six-tier neophytes to geriatric reincarns. Many guests wear facade-masks: beaming bald Eisenhowers, handsome Kennedy stereotypes, lush Cleopatras, Jean Harlows.

Jonas and Carol are exchanging conjugal emovectors with a tall geriatric couple when the music begins in the main ball room. Hanging-standing at eye level in the graviton field, the children feel routine sociometic equity. The programmers keep the sociometry optimum: absolutely no isolates, no stars (or very few stars), and no dominance-submission pairings. The orchestra eases into a Strauss waltz and the couples flow onto the floor, circling, rotating like flowers in a whirlpool. The music builds in volume and compositor coverage, and Jonas feels that he himself is producing the music—symmetric music, thesis and antithesis, call and answer, thrust and parry, implicit antiphonality—the effect tailored for flowing movement and opulent settings. The sitar is for a Hindu temple, he thinks, a Flentrop organ for a reverberent stone church, a big band for a hotel roof, and a jazz trio for a cognoscenti club.

"Anybody naked yet?" Carol asks.

"Party's barely started," Jonas says, his eyes sweeping the vistas of dancers, "the waltz is tame and introductory——"

"Strauss is savage, sensual, lustful," Carol says in lilting bell-tones, "nothing is more amorous or flirtatious than *Der Rosencavalier*."

"Swooning, soaring, ingratiating," Jonas agrees. As the music swells, the couples levitate, moving like ice-skaters on a huge carousel. The sounds soar, hang precariously in golden acoustic space, then resolve in a prolonged crescendo. A flaring major chord ends in ten seconds of reverberation, and the dancers applaud and bow. A tableau follows.

A Flagstaff clone sings lieder selections, and the concept of woman as a "tender, warm, smiling divinity" is emovectored to the guests in Mozart samples. A Carmen condensation projects its sex-infusion, some Debussy fairly sighs with sensuality, and the pathetic frustration of love comes through in Petrouchka. Soul-moving, apotheotic, carnal love scenes blossom on the compositor as Tristan and Isolde excerpts are played.

"Our own hearts beating close, one upon the other," Carol whispers, squeezing Jonas's hand.

Jonas yields to the emotionality of the moment, as samples of Cole Porter and Gershwin and Rodgers flow from the orchestral pit. The performance moves on to South American rhythms, Storeyville jazz with Jelly Roll and Fats, the instrumental virtuosity of Benny Goodman, and an interesting flashback of sticky, frog-like sexuality in a Shostakovitch excerpt. The evolutionary tableau ends with samples of Sarah Vaughn, Peggy Lee ("amorous, meaningful pout"), Lena Horne, and the romantic operettas of Herbert, Lehar, Romberg, and Friml. The guests applaud and cheer and throw flowers. The sociometric programmers sit in wall-boxes, like chaperones, beaming in changing vectors, and the dancing resumes.

"I suppose we'll get some brand of action tonight," Carol says lightly, sitting with Jonas, a Negroid couple, and two geriats.

"The same old aggression bit, I should say," the geriat woman says, sipping port, "or perhaps we'll see something truly innovative."

"I dug the Leda and the Swan show at the L.A. ruins," the black man says, leering at his consort. Jonas sips torpedo juice and citric acid and reaches for the program cube. He places it in the center of the table and it activates, glowing like a huge, faceted diamond. The six people lean in and watch as the reading appears: OLFACTORY REGIMEN.

"Hey, the smellies!" the black man says.

"The odor of my beloved," his consort sighs, making

slow panther-like movements, then lowering her head to his lap.

"The dog is aroused by the smell of the bitch," Carol says, playfully.

"Pity the fellow who leaves no scent," the geriat man says, lifting his glass.

"Fecal perfume!" Jonas says.

"Naughty microsmatic stud!" Carol sings, "and anyway, scatological dynamics are old hat."

"Childish fixation. Olfactory masochism," the geriat man says.

"Hyperbole," Jonas says, "I'm just joshing."

"Josh on, man," the black says, "you're beginning to talk my primordial smell-jazz."

"A possible clue to analinctus," the geriat wife says, her comment incongruent with her dried-leaf appearance.

"Really, my dear——" the husband says.

"Inhibitions, inhibitions," Carol teases, patting the man's bony thigh.

"Henry Miller writes of the smell of fresh cunt," Jonas says.

"Orificial nectar," Carol coos.

"Well, leave a kiss within the cup. . . ."

The olfactory cues beam in, and the dance floor half fills with cake-walkers in flapper costumes, the band blaring out Chicago jazz. A very young Fatha Hines clone smiles from a white piano as he prowls the bass keys in widespread walking tenths.

A sociometric shift, and Jonas and Carol are at another table, beside several children about their age. The talk is first light and ritualistic, complimentary, playful, then intellectually probing, communicatively incremental, cumulative, exponential. Carol and a tiny blonde girl chat about desserts, heroines, and pelvic implants. Jonas finds himself in a bothersome antagonistic pairing with an aesthenic boy. He knows cognitively that the pairing is purposive, has sociometric rationale, but his emosensors begin to flare at the boy's baitings, infinite regress questions, and verbal tours de force.

"I hate seeing you sit so close to Carol," the boy says, a one-sided smile on his flat face, "you're so existential you don't care what anybody says about you."

"Why do you let him talk to you that way?" a dark child asks Jonas.

"Oh, let him free-associate," Jonas replies, leaning back in his chaise.

"It's just because the boy is skinny," another observes.

"If I were you, I'd regress, and bust his ass," a barrel-torsoed boy whispers.

"We could use some new socioprogrammers," Carol says, her voice calm and subtle in encouraging Jonas to dislodge the skinny boy.

The thin boy looks unruffled by the comments, looks away casually at the dancers, positioning himself to block Jonas's view.

"Would you alter the angle of your regal head just ever so?" Jonas says, placing his hands on the boy's head, like a barber.

The boy cringes affectedly, like a Brahmin being touched by a Pariah. "I am advising you to remove your spuriously elite and grubby little hands," he says in measured, taunting tones.

"How'd you like to step outside?" Jonas whispers. The girls talk louder and the band plays Rosetta.

"Your teleporter or mine?"

"Tandem. On the veranda."

Jonas removes his hands and the skinny boy adjusts his wing-collar. Carol cuts a knowing look at the socioprogrammers. "Hurry back," she tells Jonas, her casual tone flicked by anxiety.

Outside, the two six year-olds face each other, looking like boys getting ready to swap marbles. "This will be a stand-off, you know," Jonas says, "and in one way or another, you must defer to my peer status."

"You're just stuffed with more gimcracks than I am," the boy waves Jonas off, "anyway, I don't care about you or your status. I want Carol. That's the whole bit. I'm applying for conjugational access to her."

"She doesn't dig pimply-faced kids," Jonas says, feeling an edge of jealousy.

"Come on, monogamy of any sort is corny. We all can have each other—unless you're some kind of neurotic maladapt. You know that."

"Don't you have a consort, little man?"

"Three," the boy leans in to Jonas, "plus a homoboy and a nympho-ewe."

"Little-ass tomcat, aren't you," Jonas says, "I think you're out of your little league, though. You'll probably have to stay in your own quad. Unless you can outrank me or shortcut the conjugational matrix."

"Let's have Carol decide," the boy says, "have her pop on out here."

"You know that all this was set up by the programmers, don't you?" Jonas says, vectoring in beneficent despotism.

The boy counters with an emosignal of anarchy and scorn. "They've set it up to see if you can cope with me, and I don't think you can."

"Do you agree that it would be stupid to fight?"

"I don't care. I'm a bull and I want your cow."

"It's obvious that you are a maladapt."

"Are you backing down?"

"From what, little puppy?"

"From meeeee!" the boy flares, snapping to a spread-stance, arms akimbo. Jonas tenses, probing the mocking eyes, the skinny nose, the curling thin lips.

"You're in over your head. Back off while you're fairly even in the game. Intrapeer group aggression is foolishly maladaptive. You'll need all your resources to fight off your wards, not to mention the geriat rovers ——" Jonas starts as the boy winks into nothingness. A sociometric mechovoice beams in:

YOUR COGNIZANCE OF INTRAPEER GROUP AGGRESSION AS MALADAPTIVE IN THIS SAMPLE OF CONFLICT REINFORCES YOUR STATUS. YOU MAY RETURN TO YOUR CONSORT.

Jonas looks out past the hemlock creepers and the giant plantain stalks to the distant plain, shimmering in the colors of the clustered moons. The foliage rustles with tiny marmots, and tawny gnarled birds lumber through the cypress groves. A steamyacht boils across the plain, its bow glowing red, and the stern billowing thunderheads of beautiful steam clouds. The reverie pops like a bubble and Carol is beside Jonas.

"Where's the little creep?" she asks.

"Zapped back by the programmers, I think," Jonas says, absently, "how's the party going?"

"Fine. Good enough. Coming back?"

"Do we have to?" Jonas bites into the moment, feeling his strengths focalize, like chrome pistons and diamond drill-points held in glistening abeyance.

"You're reading my estrovectors, darling," Carol says with a kind of sweet urgency. "I want to make love more than I want to live."

The children embrace and their clothing defluxes, revealing bodies glowing with the ventral contact, like marble turning to rosy flesh, two statues coming to life.

Pure tactile and somesthetic cues flood their sensoria, the blood drawn inexorably downward to the sacral bowls.

By a wall laced with heavy ivy, the children secure locktight coupling, Jonas feeling his pikestaff swell grandly in the downy uterine folds. Little love-making sounds mix with implant sounds: hypothalamic suckings, fulcrum clicks, neuronal buzzing, pressurized sluicing and whirring. An electric aura-sphere forms around them and the stars begin a slow distant chiming. Jonas cries out to the heavens and a hundred thousand meteorites blast from him in shuddering paroxysms.

Carol grasps his shoulders and her eyes burn with luminescence. Fleshy cilia beat in her sacral labyrinths and her sheath constricts on the shaft like a velvet pump-sleeve. She turns the teleoport bezel for 1000 feet vertical, and she and Jonas float in wispy moist clouds. Jonas stiffens as a second crystal-clear orgasm germinates, buds, and flowers at the base of his spinal chord, all geysers, throbbing pelvic floors, and swimming strabismus. Carol sobs as the third, and implantational paroxsym welds them together.

Deep in the uterine cosmos, the glistening head of a meteorite buries itself in custard ovular epithelia, and a new life bursts into being. A serene glow spreads over Carol. "We've done it, Jonas," she says softly, "we'll have a little one soon."

They beam up a flitter and drift over the tree tops, holding each other with new wonder and tenderness. The moon cluster sets and the two small children fly into the rosy dawn toward the teleport station.

XIX

"We've had our little fling, haven't we?" Carol teases Jonas, lowering a fat koala bear clone on his glowing trig puzzle. "Old before our time, square putative parents at age six yet."

Jonas deactivates the puzzle and strokes the bear. "The little monster—no, the darling cherub—won't be here for another two months, and we'll have another six years before we really have to be wary of it."

"It's going to be a little stud-boy," Carol says, a whisk of scorn in her pride.

"You know that already?"

"The readouts came from materno-central today. There's no nucleolar satellite in the chromosomal matrix. That equals masculinity. And the tiny bundle already has a genital tubercle, testis cords, and primitive kidneys."

"A solid implant then?"

"120,000 count, my lusty implanter, and one wriggler beat out all the rest."

"You know, this is an untestable hypothesis, but do you realize what the odds were *against* you and me being conceived at all? We are both winners in a race with at least 100,000 losers. We are both distinctive, as well as big fat potential zeroes——"

"Fruitless hindsight speculation. You and I are real real real——"

"And a flicker away from zilchood. I damn near got gunned down today by a geriat roverpak."

"Aren't we high on the invincibility rankings?"

"Centile 92 and still a little to go."

"Do you have all the Peer Status implants?"

"Very nearly all. I'm requisitioning extra kva for the teleporter, and minimizing the combative gimcracks. I'd rather be able to pop away than have to trade stun-bolts with some overcompensatory stud."

"Come see the tiny thing," Carol says, defluxing her sheath, her body like alabaster tinted with dark sun-light. Jonas X-rays the slightly swollen abdomen and looks in at the fetus: spinal vertebrae, the head begin-ning to form, a heart, a tail, extremity nubs.

"The face will be complete in a few days," Carol says. "Do you think he will be handsome?"

Jonas kisses the soft distended belly. "He'll be a dandy boy—hey, you're giving off beautiful raw smells, you lovely child."

"They go straight to your pikestaff, don't they?"

"Yummy, yes," Jonas says, sniffing and nuzzling the velvet skin.

"Life has to go beyond orgasms, doesn't it, Jonas?" Carol says, reflectively.

Jonas feels the aversive emovector and adjusts his tumescence downward. He kisses Carol's forehead. "Life has pinnacles, nadirs, and vast goddam blocks of fuzzy nondescriptness," Jonas sighs. "If we get canalized on the structure and function of our lives, we can get com-pressed into dialogues of despair. Except for intellective flexing, and maybe fattening our info banks yet a little more, speculating on life is maladaptive."

"I guess I'm sobered by the pregnancy," Carol says, stroking her stomach. "The little thing already seems to be tough and predatory. If I am the biologic host, this tiny angel is the ultimate parasite."

"You need some happy gas, baby," Jonas says, palm-ing on the trivid newscast. Frank Blair, a personality from the days of 2-d television, had died at age 208, a longevity record; the methane trenches at Wheeling had caught fire again; and the Chicago Robot Sox were winners of the World Series of plasmaball.

Carol palms her trivid to the distaff channel: on one facet, a fresh, delicate Millay holobot is reading *Renascence* and a white mink show is on another. Carol pops an amphet blatter into her forearm and begins to sing in trills and warbles. She dials a Himalayan cat and hugs it. Jonas smiles as she dials another, then five, ten, twenty cats, their mews and purrings filling the air.

"Suppose I dial just one giant mastiff?" Jonas laughs.

"Oh, don't, dear——"

"Of course I won't—you make a lovely picture." He crawls into the furry mass and Carol squeals with delight. The children hug each other, and the cats pad around and over and under them. The air smells of incense, freon, and tanned leather. Outside, a provobot sled notches into the pneumolock and the ingress chime sounds.

Carol suddenly looks alarmed. "Whoever could that be?" she asks, getting up and toggling the monitor, "goddam provobots——"

"Routine, I suppose," Jonas says, walking toward the port.

"No, wait," Carol says, "can you read them?"

"They're deputies," Jonas replies.

"What locus?"

"Quasoids. Mechanical messenger boys," Jonas says lightly. "What's wrong?"

"They couldn't extradite us, could they?" A flicker of alarm registers deep in Jonas's memory banks—the clone Carol left of herself at her putpars' quarters. So that was it. Somebody knew that Carol was not dead.

"Be casual," Jonas says, "play with the cats, and get by an airshaft. If you have to, pop somewhere, and beam me later." Jonas walks to the ingress port as the chime sounds again. He irises the vesicle open and faces two mesomorphic forms. Their physiogs are like welders' masks, and their slate-gray uniforms seem painted on their wooden-doll bodies. Shock-sticks sprout from their ball-socketed extremities.

"Civil census deputies, sir," one says in neutral mechotones. "May I check your identity cube?" Jonas extracts a small crystalline cube from a mastoid niche and snaps it in the bot's thoracic slot. A dim red visobar glows and the cub pops out. Jonas refits it behind his ear, emovectoring conformity and peer-level superordinacy.

"Is your consort in?" the bot asks.

"She is ill-disposed," Jonas says, "in the pregnancy regimen. She is asleep." The second bot's visual agates scan the room. Carol is lying by a lift-tube. She is in an amniotic somnobag, tucked in a fetal curl. "We have some double readings on your consort's identocube, coinciding with some readings on a pediat decedent. Kindly code in verificatory data as specified in this mandate." The bot hands Jonas a cube.

"Can this wait until she awakens?" he asks, striving for emocontrol in his voice.

"Specified time limit two hours," the bot answers, "such matters are not without precedent, and are within routine investigatory limits."

"I'll take care of it," Jonas says. The bots spin on castered podiatric bearings and move off. The port closes, and Jonas stands there, looking at the smooth verticality of the panel.

"What do we do now?" Carol vectors across the room.

"The archival cameras may be on," Jonas vectors back, "feign somnolence for awhile, or take a blinko shot. I need some time to think."

"Christ, I just blatted in an amphet."

"Well, cool it as best you can till I check the archival circuits." Jonas walks to the central console and scans the panels: energy, heat, refrigeration, illumination, water, foodstuffs, garmentage, transportation, trivids, holography, data storage. . . .

"The archival circuits are off," he says, "I think the only time they come on automatically is when life systems stop."

"Well good," Carol sighs, "the damn thing came out on the roof when we zilched Jason. It could be anywhere—do you think we're being taped?"

"I don't think so, but our retinographs could be used in any case, if we get in trouble with the Synod." Carol defluxes the somnobag, and it collapses, compressing into a tiny packet. "The baby feels restive," she says, walking slowly along the curved walls, looking out at the megalop spires in the distance. "So, we have two hours to do something."

"Do you want to stay with me?" Jonas asks, looking away.

"Of course I do," Carol says softly, an almost conjugal warmth-tone in her voice.

"But what about your feelings—I mean, about love, monogamy, sexual accessibility, the corniness of monogam life. . . .?"

"I feel mellowed about them all," Carol says. "We're changing, Jonas. We must be growing, or evolving in some way——"

"It's our psychic metabolism—hey, here's the cube. I forgot about it." He notches the cube in a refractor and the mechovoice begins:

CAROL III REX 246A, CONSORT TO JONAS SUM X 37A IS LISTED ON NECROLOGIC AS WELL AS LIFE SYSTEMS ROSTERS. PROBABILITY ERROR IS .0001 CONFIDENCE LEV-

EL. PENALTIES FOR WILLFUL DUPLICATION OF STATUS LISTINGS ARE REVOCATION AND RE-ALLOCATION OF CREDIT LINES AND/OR REHABILITATIVE DEPORTATION. CODE IN EXPLANATORY DATA OR SURRENDER TO SYNOD AUTHORITIES.

"I knew the odds," Carol says, glum-faced, despite the amphet effects, "but I couldn't stomach being sent to that goddam deportation trench at Bayonne. At least we've had some good times together."

"There may be a way out," Jonas says, "but my thinking is getting so orthodox that I get the cognitive dissonance signals."

"It's all that sub-liminal jazz beaming in from the Peerage Banks. Of course, it's clear that I should surrender, but I'm not going to. And, it's also clear that you have to turn me in. What way out is there?"

"Make a run for it." Jonas paces the deck, hands behind his back. Carol hugs her knees and rocks back and forth, the kittens still playing around her. Jonas cuts off the Bizet C Major Symphony, with its jetting compositor spires and Jack-in-the-box histobars. He dials some Scriabin and watches the wafer-thin asymmetric smoke undulate from the compositor. "I want to stay with you," he says in a soft firm voice, "and that wish immediately compromises my position as a Peer. But all the cognitive clarity I have dissolves in my autonomic reaction to you."

"Darling Jonas," Carol says, running to him, "I'm so sorry, and I'm so happy too——"

"We'll have to abdicate," Jonas says in measured tones. "We'll have to do the nomadic bit, and hope to get an early stake somewhere before our strengths run out."

"Well, let's get cracking," Carol says, "if the die is cast, you, me, and the little one here have to bundle our collective asses out of here."

"We'll take the big flitter out to the San Diego buttes," Jonas says, "we can camp there for a few days before the provobots send a sled that far. If there's any analogy here, any strategem, it's like a gambler cashing in all his chips and traveling light. We'll make ourselves into compressed powerpaks—like tiny radium blocks with energies sufficient to last indefinitely."

Jonas requisitions the Continental range flitter and codes in a one-tier checklist of supplies: wide-spectrum nutrients, extra fuel cells, phasers, and an entire life-systems console. He watches the goods and services tabulators flick out the readings, the totals building toward a saturation limit. The charbot moves about the room, securing the various controls, programming the billet for standby. The Goldberg Variations play softly in the transducer, and the silver flitter gleams in the sunflare, the delta stabs tense and ready.

Carol looks sad as the kittens dematerialize and the furniture pieces niche into the bulkheads. The children sit in charging pods and watch the isochronon spin off the minutes. Within their small bodies, the cumulative energies build toward asymptote. "Like a blast of vitamins to last a century," Carol laughs.

XX

"This is it, baby," Jonas says, defluxing his cranial shell.

Snake-like umbilici drop away from the charge-points, and the children stand up, softly crackling auras around them. They cross supply bandoliers across their small chests and life-support belts around their waists. They carry helmets and mini-computes. Implant and prosthete lids cover their bodies. They walk across the room and iris the airlock, settling carefully down into the deep contoured seats of the flitter. Jonas punches in a routine intramegalop flight plan and activates the drive. The launch pedestal telescopes out, rotates, and clicks to the azimuth reading. "Off for a day in the country," Jonas says, "and with a fat picnic basket!"

The flitter planes off, the needle-nose lifting and cleaving the air. Carol looks back, watching the billet-piston lower into the plasticrete, the antennae folding like old umbrellas. "Home sweet home," she says.

"Home is where you hang your implants," Jonas says. "We have a lot of territory to be imperative about now."

Below, the leviton trenches glow a bright sienna, and the commuter pods hiss through the tubes, like gelatin bullets in howitzer barrels. The flitter banks around a mile-high data bank monolith covered with robot scrapers and oilers. A squadron of truffle-grid copters whirl by, their paddle-rotors beating noisily. A provobot cruiser skies in beside the flitter, exchanges routine identification signals, then banks away, the robopilot saluting.

Carol feels an autonomic emoflare, but Jonas is reassuring. "He saluted the Peer medallion on the cowl," Jonas says.

The landscape flows beneath: thousands of abandoned, vandalized homes, burned-out factories, railyards sprayed with cosmoline fiber and plastifoam, hybrid camphor and eucalyptus forests crowding over ancient freeways; the vast expanses of bleached tundra, white and sterile from radiation. The broken arch over the St. Louis port looks like a huge wishbone, breaking, caught in still-action camera sequence. Huge municipal geodesics lay like bubbles on algae ponds.

Jonas booms the flitter up to 10,000 feet, and sets a course for the California islands. Ahead, the Kansas City crater blooms with wildly luxuriant foliage, and the Wichita geriatric domes gleam a wet photosynthetic green. The flitter skims the 14,000 foot summit of Pike's Peak, the sides of the mountain jumbled with millions of old automobiles, 747's, C5A clones, and flitters. Carol sings all three voices of a Bach trio sonata as the flitter blasts off the Utah National Desert at Mach 2.5. The Nevada Plain slips past, orange and rust-colored, split with fissures and epicenter radiates. The Sierra Nevada Channel looks oily and restive, after apocryphal earthquakes created a geology like that of New Zealand. Mossy green volcanic knobs dot the new and uncertain waters, where spiny mountain ridges of solid stone once rose thousands of feet into the air. Mojave Lake gleams blue and silver. The Burbank Spire has begun to list slightly. The flitter dips down to skim the concrete plains of old Los Angeles, then following the ridge of tortured keys south: past the Long Beach Game Preserve, the elephant seal colony at Laguna, the Camp Pendleton Military Graveyard, and the guano islands of Carlsbad and La Jolla.

The San Diego buttes appear ahead, like huge elephant feet, truncated and flat-topped, set in the strangely restive new waters. Jonas skims the flitter low over groves of sequoia and teak, lichen fields, and clusters of huge toadstools. He sets a glide-path over a marvelously green expanse of creeper grass, beaming in exploratory signals. He hovers the craft 50 feet over a recreation dome and opens the canopy. The air is sweet, with an elusive tic of pungency. The craft settles on to the grass, the delta stabs retract, and the force-field activates.

"Can't have any natives chopping up the Piper Cub," Jonas laughs, "let's see what's inside the dome."

The children approach the small geodome, and Jonas thinks of Hansel and Gretel discovering the cake and candy house of the witch. The dome is about 20 feet high at its peak and 60 feet in diameter. The cover of clear taut skin stretches over a basketweave frame of light metal. The dome looks clean and new, though partially covered by Bermuda grass runners. Jonas turns the free-knob and looks inside.

"We can use this without coding in anything to the data banks," he says, "but we can probably do better ourselves."

"Not exactly plush," Carol says, remembering the Christ-what-a-dump remark from some obscure cinema heroine. "I feel like I want to build a nest, Jonas," she says, seriously, "and I can feel the baby growing every hour. I think I can actually feel the cells dividing and doubling. It's exciting and erotic and somesthetic all at once. And I'm beginning to feel protective of him, and, would you believe it, I feel maternal!"

"You're a lovely Madonna."

"And you're my immaculate conceptor."

"And we're both in happy exile."

"Does anybody live around here?" Carol asks, sitting

cautiously on a soft inflated chaise. Jonas scans the dials of a small console and toggles a control:

WELCOME TO SAN DIEGO RECREATIONAL BUTTE NUMBER TWENTY-SIX. ALTITUDE FIFTY FEET, TEMPERATURE RANGE 55-67, ANNUAL RAINFALL 24 INCHES, AREA 2.9 SQUARE MILES. INHABITANTS ARE SIX JAPANESE PRIESTS AND ONE PORTUGESE TUNA FISHERMAN. THESE PEOPLE ARE GRANTED ASYLUM AND ARE PROTECTED BY STATUTE. PRIMARY RECREATIONAL FUNCTION IS REINFORCEMENT OF HOMEOSTATIC BALANCE. 100 EARTH TREMORS ARE RECORDED ANNUALLY IN THIS AREA. LEVITATION IMPLANTS ARE ADVISED. DIAL FOR EXTENDED DATA.

"Exile is the right word," Carol says, "how close are we to the continental force-field? And, can we get through it if the provos try to extradite us?"

"We should be nestled right next to it," Jonas says, "and the flit can ram it easily. It'll be like flying through a bubble-thin membrane. Just remember, baby, one delicious wrench of the teleport bezel, and we can pop halfway back to Watkins Glen. I doubt that the provos will bug us, though, this isn't the only continent on the globe. Now, let's make ourselves a lovely little nest."

The children leave the small dome and walk leisurely back to the flitter. Jonas sets up the life-systems console, and strikes an affected pose, like an organist poised over the manuals of a giant theater organ.

"First, I'll have a lovely expanse of carpet," Carol says, her finger arched casually on her cheek, her elbow resting in her palm. "How about a simple 9 x 12 for a starter?" Jonas says, rubbing his hands together.

"Deep red pile, in tight clusters please. And annealed

with matched serging," Carol replies, with mock specificity. The floor materializes. "And I'll have a cute little valve-stem chaise, all clear and lucoid and shimmery, and a teak chest, with bon-bons in a crystal dish."

"Conspicuous consumption," Jonas chides, "we could be naked and sunburned and looking for roots to chew on."

"And environdials all around, thank you. Beige velvet on one, warm yellow mohair on another, and, let's see, a wall of Dégas, and another of Aztec masks."

"And what will madam have for a ceiling?"

"Murky blue, with mammalian cloud-globes—oh, how lovely! can we keep it?"

"It'll cost a centile rank every 24 hours, my dear, and you don't have many furnishings yet."

"Well I want a pedal harpsichord in the corner."

"Extravagant child, you choose to place lovely artifacts all around you." The children sit in the tiny structure and look at each other with wonder and vague sadness.

Carol stirs, almost irritated. "I need to feel better," she says, popping a euphorion spansule into her arm. "That's better already—Christ, just think what you can do by getting goodies in your bloodstream. Now let's go exploring. We can shelve this setting." The little structure de-materializes and the children stand in the grass, looking innocent and small.

"Let's just walk," Carol says, "we always jet or flit or whisk around, I forget what the graviton loading feels like."

Jonas nods, notching a pedometer into the teleport bezel. "If we have to zap back, we'll be right at the flitter."

The creeper grasses are thick and damp, and fat grubs writhe beneath the latticed green spread. The grass gives way to a boulder field, the children climbing and levitating easily over the shale-strata of grayish stones. They walk slowly through a cluster of the huge toadstools, fleshy white trees crowned by open parachutes of ribbed yellow.

"Watch out for elves," Jonas laughs.

"Speaking of elves," Carol says softly, "what hath God wrought ahead?"

Jonas does not look right away. "It would have to be Jap priests, or one Portuguese fisherman," he says, opting to 7X visual mag, and beaming out emosensors. About 100 yards into a grove of teak trees, six short men stand in a small circle around a crude altar. Their bald heads are bowed, feet almost primly together, coarse robes hanging like heavy opera house curtains. A wavering line of incense smoke drifts up into the darkness of the small grove. The emosensor readings are distinctive: passivity, serene stupefaction, bovine stolidity, tranquility, fringe drug effects.

"They're about as close to nirvana as anyone ever gets," Jonas says.

"Maybe the Portuguese is back at the ranch meanwhile, filleting tuna."

"Or maybe they won't let him dig their deities," Jonas says.

The children come closer to the group, and stand silent. Sluggish waves slosh against the mossy sides of the butte, and the wind sings tentative little dissonances in the trees. One of the men turns and approaches the children. His face is like translucent parchment, the eyes profoundly kind, the mouth open slightly, the gait passive, almost apologetic. The man stops and bows. "Welcome to our small home," he says softly, "what will you have of us?"

"Greetings," Jonas replies, "we are touristing, recreationers, explorers."

"So young," the priest says, a kind of deference and admiration flowing into his tones. "Are you among the invincibles?"

"We are impervious to most forms of attack."

"You come in peace then?"

"Of course." The short exchange dies away, as if introductions and cognitive resolutions were now complete. Jonas realizes that both he and Carol are changing more rapidly than ever. He remembers the gleeful sadism of his recent youth, feelings which seemed soaringly right, excellent in their simplicity, unencumbered by sentimentality. He remembers Carol drawing her talons across Jason's neck, the summated stunbolts, the stark functionality of open aggression. He feels now a kind of sponge-like receptivity, a catholic compassion, a rising kindness.

"What do you do here?" Carol asks the priest.

"We are attempting to slow the passage of time, and to be one with the universe, to be one with nature as we find it here." Carol looks puzzled and vaguely amused. She wonders about solar time, psychological time, chronometer time, ovulation time. . . .

"No," the priest says. "I mean no facetious reply. We, the six of us here, left the Corporation of Japan after the completion of the 5th continental level. Our temples were buried beneath five layers of living plastic hives stuffed with people. We requested exile and were granted it immediately. 700 people applied for the six coffins we forfeited. Here we live in more space than we have ever known. It is a most pleasing life."

"I should think you would get bored," Carol says. "Doesn't time drag horribly?"

The priest smiles, he seems infinitely patient. "Our

precise goal is to slow the passage of time. We cannot alter the orbital velocity of the planet, nor the spinning rate. We cannot prolong the sunlight or shorten the darkness. But we can seek a rhythm of activity that feels good and best and natural. We do this by removing all ritualistic restraints based on psychological time. We have no chronometric schedule and no societal impingements of time. We eat and sleep and meditate whenever we wish. We seek the perfect life rhythm."

"What do you do for kicks?" Carol persists. "Like, do you do sex?"

"We are eunuchs," the priest says, unabashed. "We should be infinitely more troubled if the rhythms of continence intruded on us. Tell me, are you fugitives?"

Jonas feels a mental gunfighter stance, and Carol looks decidedly guarded.

"It is not important," the priest replies softly, seeming to read the childrens' reactions precisely. "You are safe here. Few people come, and we get almost no municipal contacts whatever."

"We are fugitives," Jonas says, "but not maladapts or desperados. The Synod Conjugational Matrix wants to separate us, and we wish to remain together."

"Come eat with us at sunset, if you wish," the priest says, bowing and turning back toward the small circle of silent forms standing in the grove.

"Thank you," Jonas replies. The man seems to sift on the ground, almost levitational, Jonas thinks.

The children walk around the periphery of the butte. The air blows in restless, unresolved surges, as if the atmosphere was always expecting some placidity. To the west, the force-dome layer shimmers like a sheet of subtropical rain, fading away against the directionless canopy of the sky. A tight little echelon of flitters skims the white-caps to the south, the drivers shouting and waving at each other. To the East, the buckled humps of new rock and knobs of moss and fungi dot the waters, and across the upwater channel, domes and spires are dimly seen.

"How's the little parasite doing?" Jonas asks.

"He feels like a trampoline champion, and, can you possibly guess, he has been tapping code messages to me."

"Impossible!"

"I thought so."

"Well, what the triple-assed hell is he saying?"

"Guess."

"Come on, Carol, I'm dying to know."

"Here, you can see for yourself, if you want, and try a message to him. He knows Morse and God knows what else." Carol sits beside a wet, darkly stained cedar tree. She assumes a basic yoga position, then spins slightly, and lies supine. "No tricks now," she teases, "this position feels good."

"I wonder if the little stud can see me," Jonas says, bending over Carol's body. He presses his ear against the white abdominal mound, and auto-vectors sensitive audition. Movements ripple across the stomach. The sounds from inside are ethereal, cavernous, reverberant —a spring-loaded clack in fluid resonance, low crisp mutterings, gutteral snorts, sluicing, pressurized spumes, hydraulic licking, valves, capstans, fulcrums, winches, hoists, kingposts. Jonas draws a teasing little mandala around the area, and feels the baby react. He listens again, determined not to x-ray just yet. He pictures himself listening at some massive door, motionless and tense, and an adversary listening on the other side, hoary espionagic faces a bare inch from one another. He chuckles at the slapstick scene, and taps in a little message:

HELLO THERE IN THE SWEET NEST. THIS

IS YOUR BIG DADDY-BOO, SAYING GOOD WISHES AND HOPE YOU ARE DOING WELL. YOUR LOVELY MOTHER SAYS YOU KNOW CODES. SO TAP US BACK A MESSAGE.

Jonas repositions himself, snuggling luxuriously against the ripe belly-globe, and reaches for Carol's hand. The tapping begins. It is rapid and steady, advanced Galactic Morse derivative:

IF YOU THINK SWALLOWING AMNIOJUICE ALL DAY IS FUN, YOU'RE OFF YOUR CEREBRAL GOURD, AND THE NEST IS SALTY AND ALKALIDE, NOT SWEET. AND HELLO DADDY. I CANNOT SEE YOU BUT YOU FEEL OKAY. I FEEL READY TO GET THE HELL OUT OF HERE, EXCEPT THAT THE TEMPERATURE IS NICE, AND IT'S ALL SPONGY AND WEIGHTLESS AND SHOCK-ABSORBED. AND THERE ARE GIMCRACKS AND COMPUTES AND LEADS SNAKING ALL OVER THE PLACE. HOW MUCH LONGER?

Jonas's face reads disbelief, strange, wild joy, then asymmetric dismay. "He sounds like a predator already," Jonas's voice sounds whining.

"The readouts show 187% parametric growth increments. I didn't want to complicate things by worrying you."

Jonas x-rays the area and stares in disbelief. The child is fully formed, lying supine, eyes open, pupils dilated, the face set in a remarkably purposive stare. The arms are folded across the chest, the fingers drumming impatience. The child looks like a man tolerating a steambath or waiting for a rainshower to let up.

"God, they must come out ready to fight," Jonas says. "He looks good, but far from cuddly."

"I'd swear he tweaked me deep in the ass this morning. My first internal goose—a real live intra-uterine postillión."

"He wants to know how much longer."

"I know, baby."

"Well?"

"About five days for me. He's ready right now, but I'm not, unless you want to do some serging and annealing and patchwork aperturition repair."

"Any other alternatives? Can't we induce labor?"

"You can try bouncing on me."

"Be serious——"

"No, I mean, you can do the old artificial respiration bit topsy-turvy. It'll amount to abdominal contractions, and you can bet your paternal ass that the little stud will be clawing at the exit ramp." Carol codes in a message:

BABY BE PATIENT WE WILL TELL YOU EVERYTHING YOU WANT TO KNOW CAN YOU SEE ANYTHING WE CAN BEAM IN SOME TRIVIDS TO HELP PASS THE TIME

THANKS LOADS SOLAR TIME PERCEPTION NO PROBLEM CENTRIFUGAL CUES SUGGEST TERRESTRIAL VELOCITY AT 20 MPS PSYCH TIME IS WORSE BUT NOT CRITICAL I CAN DO SOME SUBVOCALIZING SO DROP THE CODE

"Impossible," Jonas breathes, arms akimbo, head shaking. "Do you mean to say that we have spawned a superbright?"

"You are just as right as rain, big poppa Joanie."

"Well, what the hell are we going to do?"

"You are going to gather hot water while I parturiate him."

"He may turn on you the minute he gets clear."

"Shit, I wanted to suckle him."

"This ought to be a happy event, shouldn't it?"

"There's nothing happy about dropping a brat—it's like shitting a brick."

XXI

"You know, Carol, coming here may turn out to be a wise, a symbolic, or even a religious event," Jonas says, seeming to want to share some vague secret enthusiasm.

Carol walks beside the softly rounded cliff edges, arms crossed over her stomach. She stops and sits on a moss clummock. "That sounds pretty, baby, but the parturition bit coming up is not going to be so pretty. We—I—have to do a birthing, you know, a whelping, a hatching——"

"Cast naked upon the naked earth——"

"God, I'm worried about episiotomy tears, and you're spouting poetry. . . ."

"I'll help you all I can, baby, in fact, I was thinking that the birth could come off better here, than back at Materno-Central. In a way, we're like Mary and Joe humping the jackass into Egypt to drop JayCee in the stall."

"I know, you've already called me a madonna."

"What I mean is, we—you, are in a basically primitive setting. True, we've got a flitter full of gimcracks, and access to a lot more, but I was thinking you might want to do a natural birth, out here, in the open."

"Whatever *for*? I'd rather get blinkoed and wake up when all the mess is over."

"Think though, of the unnatural techniques of obstet delivery. Back at Maternocent, you'd get supine, get your lovely succulent ass elevated on a table that's too high anyway, your slim ankles would get buckled into stirrups, and then, some sadistic obstet would reach for his chrome forceps unless you had a precipitate delivery."

"I've still got a parietal stitch pattern from what the obstet called low elective forceps."

"He did the electing. And you get prepped and shuffled and shaved and molded and preened and posed ——"

"And some parchment-dry nurse would get her kicks when I started to tear."

"I'll help you, and if you get scared, or anything bad goes wrong, we can dial about anything you want. Did you ever hear about births among primitive Eskimoes?"

"No."

"I came across it on a wonderfully rare cube. An aged woman, skin like elephant hide, was telling her daughter what to do after the baby got clear. The actual parturition was simple—done in a widespread hunker squat—the way we ought to be doing it today. Anyway, the old woman said that if it was a girl, she had to stuff its mouth full of snow and slide the body far out on the ice floes. If it was a boy, bite the cord through, lick the boy all over, then rub him with whale oil and wrap him in furs."

"Why did they kill the girl?"

"They did it only if there were no male children in the family. If boys were already in the family, it was all right to keep the girl."

"That's horrible."

"I can surely identify with the girl-child. Suppose she had advanced cognition, and knew what was happening to her. Suppose she was like ours, inside?"

"The little cat's eavesdropping," Carol winces, "and he just goosed me again."

"Have you felt any contractions?"

"No."

"Be sure and tell me when they start."

"Well, I'm not going to be coy about that."

The heliofires stream down the horizon, and the red sodden globes dip into the watery vista and begin to sink immediately. Borealis streamers streak the rapidly darkening sky. The intercontinental airspace tunnels begin to shimmer their coded lights, the intracont traffic grids soar at medium altitude, and the regional mazes glow like 3-D labyrinths. The children continue to walk slowly along the rim of the butte, the sunset orange and amber on their faces.

"My life rhythm feels thrown off," Carol says, "I don't know if I'll dig this isolation for very long."

"We can put in almost any kind of experience you want, baby. Let's check the flit and go eat with the priests."

"I don't know if I want to or not."

"Come on. It will be perfectly safe, and I want to find out more about them. Look on it as a cordial invitation to dine with lovely friends."

"Six Jap priests and a fisherman aren't exactly exclusive, but I guess I'm ready."

The silver flitter sighs over the darkening butte, like an owl on feathery soft and silent wings. The sense of power and gravitational control in its flight is elusive but compelling. The air around it glows an electro-aura. Dipping over a stand of giant bamboo canes, Jonas sees the compound, a semicircle of hovels and lean-tos, set around a firepit. A huge pig is roasting over a bed of sputtering coals. Jonas eases the flitter down, all silence and taut monococque skin, glittering, glinting, a complex alien machine in a primitive setting.

"Welcome again," the priest says, "your craft is impressive. Tell me, do you enjoy mobility? Do you like soaring through the sweet ethers in a machine?" Jonas secures a force-field around the flit and notches a control pak in his thoracic recept.

"Yes," he replies, "aside from the basic logistics of having one's self transported from one place to another, the flying and teleporting is fun."

"Pleasure in the product, and pleasure in the process," the priest says, "a happy coalescence of means and ends." He motions Jonas and Carol to sit on large hemp mats. The six other men move about like servants: one turns the pig, prodding its flanks with a stick, another spreads elephant-ear fronds in front of the mats, and another pours a clear fluid into chalky white mugs. The men sit in silence, seeming to regard the children with awe and gentle deference.

"We will offer ritual to the deity we have reified," the priest says, "ambivalence of means and ambivalence of ends summates to ritualism. You may join us if you like." Carol prods Jonas, and they stand. He stands and lifts his face into the soft light. The other men stand. "We awake to find ourselves riding on a spinning primordial fleck of mud, destined to live for a time, and then to die. We offer thanks for our bodies and our senses and our cognitive strengths. Unaware of our destinies, and unaware of our goals, we strive for those processes and products which seem to be noble and natural."

One of the men carves the pig and places cubes of meat on the fronds. A tortilla-like bread is served, with spinach leaves. Carol jabs a cub with a stick and lifts it to her mouth. The clear fluid tastes like peach nectar. The men begin to eat, slowly and noisily, with overt relish, even gluttony. They belch sonorous, clittering, serrated sounds, and Carol looks uneasy. "Do you find the repast appropriate?" the priest asks Jonas, stuffing a puckered spinach frond in his mouth. "Quite good,"

Jonas says, "we are taught to suppress oral eructations, however."

"My apologies. It is our way of signifying the excellence of the food."

"Do you sometimes fast?" Jonas asks.

"Fasting is our basic practice. We eat at sunset only, and have several fasting spans during our calendrical tiers."

"I find myself wondering what brand of small talk to try with you. It's a matter of what do you say after you say hello."

"We find ourselves talking very little——"

"Like the people in Act Five of Back to Methuselah."

"I know that cube. Act Five is set in the year 35,000."

"We have outgrown, so to say, our need for semantic monitors. We know among us who trumpets, who cajoles, who scoffs, sneers, pontificates—all the rest. We accept each other and try to award each other the golden balm of silence." Jonas drains the earthenware mug and a man refills it from a tall cannister. Jonas raises the mug in a toast posture.

"Do you get drunk sometimes?"

"No. One of our beliefs is that intoxication is unnatural."

"Do you like to feel good? like, satiation is fun, eating pork is fun."

"Homeostatic balance interplays nicely, pleasingly, with satiation. I suppose we do have some gluttonous tropisms."

"And you really don't do any sex?" Carol perks in.

"No, my dear child. I remember my father telling my mother about the vesicular pressures of sex. I do not wish to offend you——"

"No, go on."

"The patterns of sex were always the same, as I recall.

Something analogous to heat, rutting, estrus peaking—call it what you will—occurred periodically, cyclically, in the females, though they never seemed to actually seek out sexual contact." The priest holds a pork-cube which is clearly phallic in shape. He smiles wanly, cuts the shaft at the center, and eats. Carol and Jonas smile. The men are silent. "My father," the priest continues, "moved persistently, relentlessly, toward my mother. He leaned toward her, gravitated toward her, devoured her with his eyes, reached out for her, smelled her, and, of course, set himself upon her sexually. He used to tease her, saying that if she had a candlestick growing between her legs, she would know how he felt, how it felt to be a man. A pipe, he would say, a cucumber, and filled with nectar under pressure. He would often vent his semen by hand, feeling perhaps, that my mother deserved some respite from his thrusting. And he came to know, after what seemed like many years, about the simple relationship of vesicular pressure to wanting sexual relief."

"Who was it that said, love ain't nothing but sex misspelled?" Carol laughs.

"I know," Jonas says, raising his hand like a student in a spelling bee, "it was that famous writer from the 20th century, Ellen Harlison."

"He was right-right-right!" the priest says, moving his hands in short arcs, "all of us here have had vesicle extirpation. There is nothing to swell our candlesticks. We are permanently and happily detumescent."

"What's the incentive to get on?" Jonas asks earnestly. "Is your motivation indegenous? do you have any self-starters . . . any signals to keep you going?"

"Of course, there are basics, like food and rest, and a kind of nirvanic homeostasis——"

"What about heterostasis?" Carol puts in.

"Evolutionarily maladaptive," the priest replies, "except for the genocidal effects it eventually generates. To seek action, take chances, be aggressive, is self-decimating. It is due, after all, to an abnormally large hypothalamus. I like the quote that bravery is a form of stupidity."

"G. B. Shaw again," Jonas says, "but how can one explain the hundreds of years of warfare, the raw fact that hostility is more prevalent, and perhaps more natural?"

"For many of the wars, the explanation is disarmingly simple—and I made an unwitting pun—international munitions cartels started them, for the simple goal of getting rich, and getting richer."

"The Arms of Krupp," Carol says.

"Dupont," Jonas says, "and Dow Chemical. Sweet little ladies driving their Datsuns to Culver City to make jellied gasoline to drop on other sweet little ladies."

"And waiting for payday, overdrawing their ready reserve, staying a month behind on mortgage payments, and two years behind on taxes," Carol says. The darkness begins to close in on the small group.

The priest looks at Carol's belly. "Would that we could incubate life," he says, almost wistful, admiringly. "We men may rule the world——"

"But the hand that rocks the cradle . . ." Carol replies.

"Ah yes. Perhaps all leaders, however powerful or cruel, pale in the presence of their spouses. But the idea of a miniature organism growing inside one's body overpowers me. Men may conquer nations, amass great wealth, fly to the stars, but, alas, we cannot have babies. Ah, the beautiful isomorphism of it! A little one, growing in your belly!"

Jonas smiles and seems to puff out his chest. "But we

are the implanters, though. The plowshares, the blades cleaving the furrow, the inundators, the seminal drenchers of the estral flames." Jonas turns to Carol and sees her face stiffen.

"I'd swear the little shit just struck a wooden match on my coccyx," she says.

"The birthing is imminent then?" the priest asks.

"Yes. Jonas, I'm not scared—not yet anyway, but I just felt something like a peritoneal mudslide. At the risk of sounding corny, I think the time has come."

"Hey, inside," Jonas speaks to the small abdominal globe, "we are ready to bring you out. Tell us what's going on in there." The men surround Carol, hushed and attentive. She remains sitting cross-legged on the mat.

HELLO BIG DADDY AND LITTLE MOTHER. THINGS ARE STARTING TO BREAK LOOSE IN HERE, LIKE A BALLOON IS COLLAPSING AND I'M INSIDE IT. I CAN SEE AN OSMOSIS METER THROUGH THE AMNIOTIC HAZE, AND IT SHOWS THE PERMEABILITY DROPPING LIKE THE PLUG'S BEEN PULLED OUT. SPEAKING OF PLUGS, HOW THE HELL DO I GET OUT OF HERE? MY UMBILICUS IS STARTING TO SHRIVEL — HEY, A BIG PERISTALSIC SHUDDER!

"Ugh, a shudder is right," Carol says, "that was an A number one contraction."

"Go by raw instinct," Jonas says, "how do you feel? do you want anything?"

"May we help?" the priest asks, "do you want privacy?"

"I feel more exhibitionistic than seclusive—I think," Carol says.

"Do you feel strong, well, operant?" Jonas asks, kneeling, and putting his hands on her shoulders.

"Yes."

"Tell us what you want."

"I'm tempted to send you all off to heat water, but I won't. First, get some big elephant-ear leaves, and make a ceremonial nest, something for the boy to get blatted on to. I'll be all right here." The men spin and run off to get the fronds, as if starting an Easter egg hunt.

ARE YOU PRETTY, LITTLE MOTHER? I WANT TO SEE YOU. I HOPE YOU LIKE THE WAY I LOOK. I HOPE TO HELL YOU DILATE ENOUGH SO MY LITTLE SOFT-BOILED SKULL DOESN'T GET SQUEEZED OUT OF SHAPE. THIS WON'T HURT—I'M GOING TO SPREAD THESE LITTLE LIPS A BIT—THERE, DO YOU FEEL ANYTHING?

"That feels good, baby. Mother's tiny intrauterine boy. I've got a checklist here you can help me with. First, do you see or feel anything that causes you to think that anything is *wrong*?"

NO I DON'T THINK SO.

"Any decidual hemorrhaging?"

WHAT'S THAT?

"Do you see any blood anywhere?"

NO.

"Hydatiform placental degeneration?"

COME ON MOM.

"Premature rupture of membranes?"

NO.

"Cord anomalies?"

MINE LOOKS BEAUTIFUL.

"Endocrine balance?"

NO SWEAT.

"Displacement or retroplacement of the uterus?"

I'M SNUG AND NICELY FITTED IN HERE.

"Any hints of trauma because of radiation, electric shock, lightning, alcohol. . . ."

NO, BUT YOU DOWNED A BLOODY MARGUERITA THE OTHER DAY THAT SCARED ME. AND BIG DADDY NEEDS TO WATCH HIS SCREWING WHILE I'M IN HERE. THE ENDOMETRIUM ENGORGEMENTS ARE FUN FOR YOU-ALL, BUT NOT FOR ME.

"Has our exodus bothered you?"

NO. I THINK IT MADE ME FEEL BETTER.

"Here come the men with some lovely soft fronds for you to land on——"

YOU'RE NOT GOING TO DROP ME, ARE YOU?

"No, baby, you'll be fine. There, Jonas, make a nice nest for the baby." The men drop the thick fleshy fronds and arrange them into a circular nest.

"Have you felt any external trauma?"

NO, BUT YOU SOMERSAULT A LOT.

"Any RH dyscrasia?"

I DON'T UNDERSTAND, MOTHER . . .

"Are there any particulates bugging you? Any gnats in the air? Any hairy pebbles?

NO, NOTHING BUT AMNIOTIC GOODIES.

"Any effacement of the cervix?"

IT'S JUST BEAUTIFUL.

"How does your metabolism feel?"

LIKE WARM GLOWING ANTHRACITE COAL.

"PBI's?"

NEAT AND TANGY AND PROTEIN BASED, JUST LIKE NEW.

"Vitaminic loadings?"

VERY NICE.

"Well, it looks like you're ready. I hope you haven't been picking at your vernix caseosa again—you'll need it for lubrication. About how long is your hair?"

ABOUT ONE INCH.

"Do you have finger and toe nails?"

YES. PROTRUDING A LITTLE.

"The circumference of your head should equal the circumference of your shoulders. Can you tell if this is so?"

NO, MOTHER.

"I'll have Jonas check that. Jonas, go get a nice lamp to hang over me—something, say, like the Bethlehem star, and maybe some strobes to light up the undersides."

"Any more pains?"

"Yes, but no crisis yet. I'd like some music, too——"

I LIKE BACH!

"Noble choice," Jonas says, "we'll try some nice little things from Anna Magdalena's book——"

I DIG CONVOLUTED FUGUES.

"How about me?" Carol asks. "Let's see, music to parturate by. I'll go along with JSB, just keep it serene, at least for awhile. I want to deliver, not be delivered." She walks toward the leafy nest. The sky is dark and silent. Carol defluxes her toga and stands nude. She walks on to the leafy fronds and stands in the center, a white pistil in a green corolla. The men murmur soft tones of awe and seem to want to worship her. Jonas approaches, also somewhat awestruck.

"Put a force-field over us, Jonas, and the light above me, and the strobes beneath. I'm going to keep my lovely pubic hairs. Stand close by me, there, face to face." Carol alters her stance, planting her feet apart, angled slightly outward, and places her arms akimbo. She looks at Jonas. "Ready?"

"My goddess of life," he says, "yes."

Carol looks at the circle of men, the softly glowing dome, the will-of-the-wisp globe above her, and the strobe lights beneath. The lights cast long shadows on her, as she begins to lower herself very slowly, hands on her knees, squatting down in a deep-settled hunker posture. As she rocks, ever so slightly, she puts her arms straight out, so that her triceps rest on her knees. Jonas lowers himself to face her.

"You may kiss the gateway of life," she says, looking steadily at Jonas. Jonas rolls supine and positions himself under Carol, kissing the labia into increased dilation.

"Now, come and lock hands with me," she says, "until the head of the new one protrudes, then, cradle the head, and help in lowering the baby to the ground." The 147 cantata begins, in beautifully controlled legato, flowing, flowing. Carol lowers her head as a contraction bulges the perineum. Jonas moves to massage the area, somehow knowing that this will prevent tearing. The bulge continues with each contraction. Soon a little of the baby's head is visible. "I want a mirror," Carol says, and Jonas quickly places one beneath her. Each contraction brings a little more of the head into view, then slowly it disappears. Now it remains visible between each contraction.

MOTHER, THE SKIN ON THE TOP OF MY HEAD IS BEING FORCED TOGETHER. . . .

"Be cool, little one, you're a rubber ball being pushed through a bottleneck."

STRETCHING, STRETCHING, PUSHING, ENERGY, PUSHING, STRETCHING . . . .

"His head is in my hands," Jonas says, tears in his eyes. The men have dropped to their knees and moved close to Carol.

GOD IT'S COLD OUT HERE. GET THIS CAUL SACK OFF MY FACE!

Jonas feels the slick head, his fingernails cannot penetrate the sack. He gets a finger under the chin and tears the sack loose.

YAY, THANKS DAD—HEY, NO KISSING!

Jonas sucks fluid from the nostrils and throat. The baby cries—a reflex cry—then a tiny voice comes out in crisp articulation: "Wipe my eyes. I want to see my mother." Jonas kisses the eyes, sucking them gently. The tiny body turns sideways, as if someone inside were turning it, and another contraction pushes the baby out on to the leaves. Carol picks him up and hugs him, the cord still attached, and still inside her.

"My lovely baby boy!" Carol says.

"You feel good, mother, but I'm still cold as hell."

"Jonas, get something to keep our boy warm."

"Beautiful," the priest says, "a religious experience, a communal joy."

"Hey, who are these chink-looking cats?" the baby flares. What have we wrought, Jonas thinks.

"What brand of world is this? Here, let me suckle this snowy breast. I can bite it, too. . . ."

"Please don't, baby."

"Daddy-boo looks moderately juvenile there—what are you cats gaping at? Go do some ablutions—you know—like, some Shintos or some Hail Marys. Go change some water into wine. Give me that towel, Dad—ah, Jonas—well, come on, what's the matter with you? Of course I can dry myself. I need to jog a little. Good old proprioception and kinesthesis. Hey, that feels good. How about some clothes? Color? I don't care. Or skip the duds and just lay an isomorph on me. How about some M and M's? Got any onion rings? Dark ale? No, not pale beer—dark ale, you know, like BOCK, the jazz off the bottom of the keg. How about changing that cantata to a fugue? Mother—Carol, baby—you turn me on. Of course I can do spermatogenisis. That's a dumb statement. Incest is just an anthropologic artifact. What better way to initiate a boy into heterosex? Hey, where are you going? Get out of the way, slant eyes. So, this is my flitter. Pretty nice. MY in the editorial sense, Jonas. Feeling possessive is corny. Besides, I'm family, right? Any sibs? Good. How about pets? Do I get my own trivid? Here, let me take the controls. I want to sit in Carol's lap. I like you nude. Why are we flying so low? Where are we going? Let me try that other tit. No, that's not my umbilicar stump, mother. Well, I can't help it if you get me tumescent. Why did we leave those guys back there? Why did you walk away from me? Hey, a shooting star! And intermeg cruisers —Hey, wait, I don't have any implants yet—no fair stunbolting—hey, dad, don't do that—OW!"

"Christ, doesn't he ever shut up?" Jonas says, placing the dazed little form on a niche.

"Ontogeny recapitulates phylogeny, dear," Carol says, "just think, you get to relive your life through your very own son."

"Happy days are here again," Jonas sighs. "The first thing we'll need is a tough materno-surrogate."

"You had to have one when you were little. You know, we are royalty without any clothes." The flitter settles down at the edge of the butte. "What will become of us? I want to hug my baby."

"We'll be growing up again," Jonas says, "and 3000 is a good tier for that."

"Come kiss me, but keep an eye on the brat."

"We'll have to go back to Oak Park, Carol."

"That will be nice, dear, will they take us back?"

"I'm sure they will. I hope they will. Anyway, we'll blast off at dawn."

"We've only been gone a few hours. Let's leave right now.

"Do you really want to?"

"Yes."

"I'm not certain how things will work out."

"Better to be prodigals than exiles."

Carol gathers the baby in her arms as the flitter hovers over the spongy turf. The craft lifts off slowly, moving over the precipice and the lapping waves. It angles gently and begins a shallow arc up into the velvet sky. The men below lift their eyes as the drive cuts in, flaring a golden borealis across the sky.